IN THE SOUTH OF TEXAS
A TOOMBS SULLIVAN ADVENTURE
BOOK SIX

TOM PILGRIM

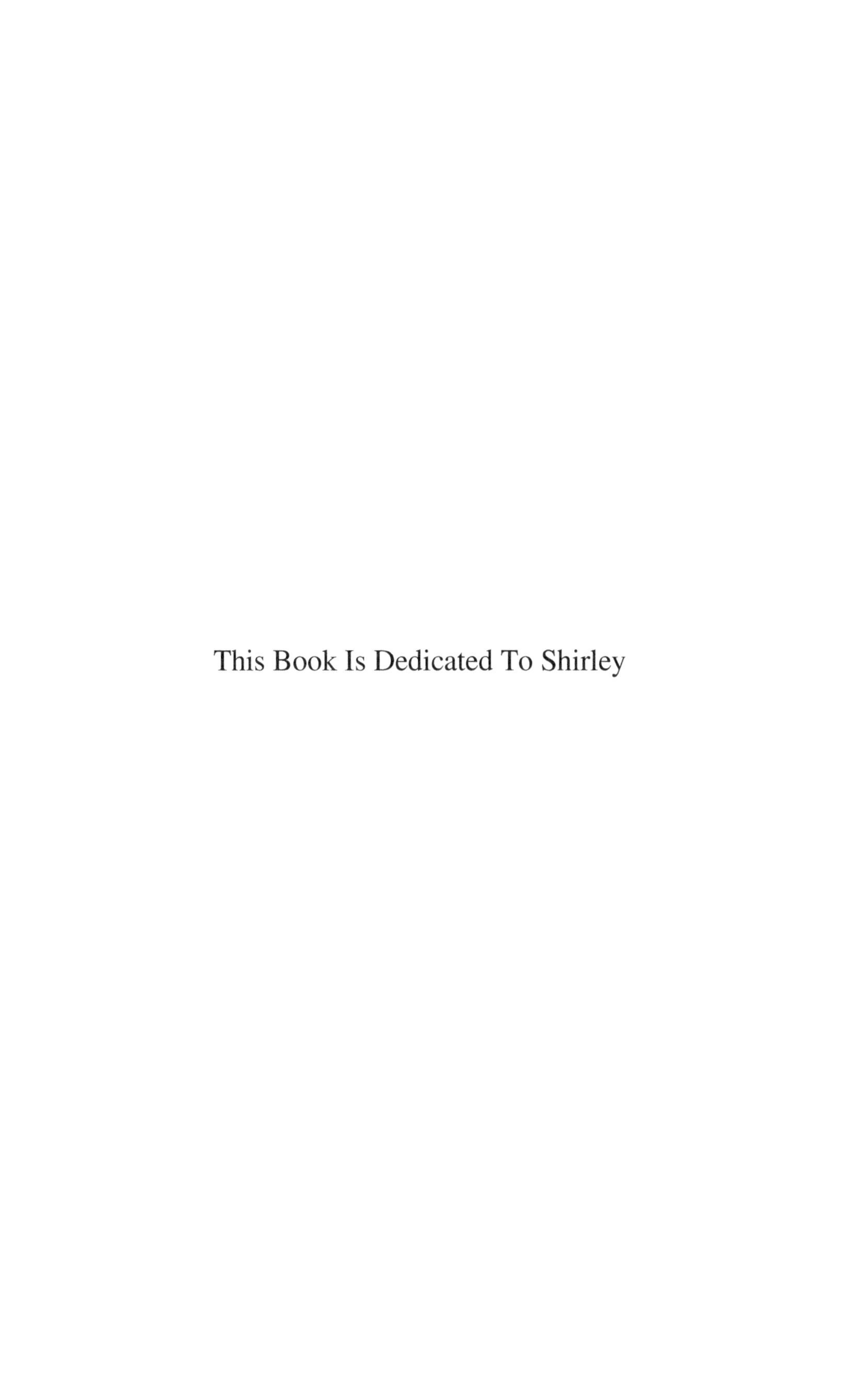

This Book Is Dedicated To Shirley

Chapter 1

Toombs Sullivan sat on his horse as he spit in the river. It was the Rio Grand, that river that is the boundary line between Texas and Mexico. He was not supposed to go across the river. He was a Texas Ranger, and had no authority, no jurisdiction, no business, and certainly no permission to cross that river. However, Sullivan had done it before. It was just that one time, but it was necessary that one time. He had gone after Nacona Pledger, the half-Indian and half-white killer, that one necessary time. And he had administered justice that one time, well-deserved justice.

He let his horse drink the river water. When the horse had had enough, Sullivan eased

him into the river. He was going across, permission or no permission. This was necessary.

The Rio Grand is a grand river indeed. It is also known as Rio Grande del Norte. It is the fifth longest river in the United States of America. It begins as a mountain stream 12,000 feet above sea level in the San Juan mountains of Colorado. That little stream then becomes the great river that flows 1,900 miles. It comes from the mountains all the way down to the fertile delta on the coast. There are places where it has high cliffs on both sides, where there are rapids, where it is wide and narrow and shallow.

Toombs Sullivan crossed the river in the far south-east corner of Texas, near Brownsville. He had been in south Texas many times. But this time it was more serious.

After being out of the Rangers for a short period of time, he had come back, and was given back his last rank of sergeant.

He had left the Rangers because of his love for Josephine Wells. He knew it would not be fair to marry her, and then be gone most of the time. It was for that reason he had become a Deputy in Fort Worth. They were married, and soon were expecting a child. Then tragedy struck as she was killed by a mad-man, a hired killer at times, and a seeker of revenge at other times. He came after Sullivan to get revenge for the deaths of several Comanches who were his friends, Comanches Sullivan had killed. Pulling himself together, Sullivan went after the killer who had lured him far away to his hide-out. There Sullivan got his own revenge.

In pursuing that man, Sullivan realized he was back doing what he had done as a Ranger, when he was tracking Indians across a vast area. He also had to admit to himself that being a town Deputy, doing little more than arresting drunks most of the time, was not for him. He was at his best doing what he loved best, being a Texas Ranger.

So now he was going after another man. He had been sent there to get him. It was no secret that years before he had gone into Mexico. If you send a man to get another man who lives in Mexico then what is expected? It made sense, really good sense, that he was in a way being given permission to cross the river. How else was he supposed to get that man he was after? You go to where that man is. You cannot just sit by the edge of the river and hope he will come there some day in the not too distant future.

Still it was not a legal thing to do. It was against the laws of the State of Texas and probably against some law of the United States of America.

Sullivan wondered what the result of all this might be. What if he provoked some international incident? That could bring the national government down hard on the neck of Texas officials who would then bring down something hard on the Texas Rangers, and he knew how these things worked. It would come down hard on his neck. He was the last man in line.

Well, he thought, he was looking for a job when he found that one. So he would just get on with it and let the Devil take the hind-most part as the old folks used to say.

Chapter 2

When Sullivan returned to Forth Worth after tracking down his wife's killer, he immediately sent a telegram to Captain Jack Rice in Dallas asking to be reinstated and sent far away south. Jack Rice was happy to have Sullivan back, asking him to come to Dallas as soon as he could.

Sullivan sold the house he and Josephine had bought, paid a few bills, and made a few arrangements with the bank about the money for the house. He also withdrew some money to hold him until he got paid again by the Rangers. In three days, he left Fort Worth for what he hoped was forever.

As Toombs Sullivan rode east toward Dallas, he could not help thinking about Constance, his first wife he thought had died during the war. But he had found her at the ranch Josephine Wells had owned. With her husband dead, she had suddenly disappeared. He was not thinking of getting back together with her for he was still in mourning, but he had loved her early in his life, so how could he not be concerned about what happened to her? Losing two women was too much for any man he thought. She was gone when he came home from the war to Georgia. There were two graves in the back of the barn at their farm. He just knew it was his wife and son. That is why he left Georgia and went to Texas, where he soon became a Texas Ranger. Finding out she was alive was a shock to him. Now she was gone again. This time he thought she was alive, but where she went, he had no idea.

He was still almost in a state of shock over recent events. He rode along almost in a trance. Soon he was in Dallas, the trip seeming to be much shorter because of him being in such deep thought.

He went straight to Captain Jack Rice's office.

"Sullivan! Come in! Come in!" Rice exclaimed, as he jumped up from his desk.

Sullivan took off his hat, stuck out his hand, and walked toward Jack Rice, who had come out around his desk.

"Glad to see you, Captain."

"I'm glad to see you, but what in the world has happened that caused you to want to come back to the Rangers? I thought you had been domesticated forever. Sit down, sit down."

"I thought so as well. But life takes its unexpected turns, don't it? Ya don't never know what tomorrow will bring to ya, good or ill. Josephine is dead. I quit my job, sold the house, here I am."

"My god, Man, what happened?"

"There was a breed over around there by the name of Comanche Joe Storm. He was a hired gun killer, but also liked to kill just for the fun of it, I guess. Anyway, he decided to get even with me because I had killed at various times and various places some of his Indian friends. He kept leaving dead animals on our back steps that related to the names of his friends. Then one night, we was staked out waiting on him to appear, me and Josephine and Sheriff Morrison, who was my boss. We had a good plan, but he was smarter. I was in the barn. He slipped into the house, killed Morrison, and took Josephine captive. I tracked them down to Josephine's former ranch. I found her dead, killed in the worst Indian way. It took me a few days, but I caught up with him at his hide-out, which is what he wanted me to do. He trapped me, but I tricked him, and killed him in the best Indian way. Having done all that, I realized town sheriffin' just ain't for me. She was gone. Nothin' to hold me there now. I knew then that I am a Texas Ranger. I can't never be nothin' else. So here I am."

"I'm so sorry about all that, Sullivan. If I was a praying man, I'd surely pray for you, but I ain't much good at it, but still, ya have my good thoughts for ya. Anyways, I'm glad you're back with us. When I got yore telegram, I sent word right on to Austin that you was back and wanted to be there again. They said come on down there, and they'd be so glad to have ya, need ya."

"Thanks. That's where I got started, ya know. They took me in untried, and gave me a chance back when I first come to Texas direct from the war. I was a lost soul wandering west and got this far. I took the defeat and the surrender bad. Got home and found my wife Constance was dead. And the boy. But she was not really dead. She and her husband, she thought I was killed in the war, had bought that ranch Josephine had owned.

When I found Josephine there, dead, Constance was nowhere around. The place was deserted."

"You have had a hard time, my friend. I hope things go better for you now."

"I guess it's just life, Captain. You have to take what comes to ya, and try to do yore best. I'm tryin'."

"I know you are. That's why the Texas Rangers will always need you and men like you. I wish you well in the south."

"Thanks. I'll be here till in the morning."

"Good. I'll buy yore supper for ya. Here's yore badge."

"Thanks. I'll wear it with pride."

With that, Sullivan left the office. He went across the street, and got a room at the hotel where he had lived for several years. As he walked into the large lobby, he thought of all the conversations there with friends, fellow Rangers, many of whom had been killed fighting Indians.

He went up to his room, put down his gear and his two rifles, the Winchester and the Sharps. He threw his hat on a chair, took off his boots, put his pistol on the table by the bed, and took off his bullet belt. He lay down on the bed. The memories came flooding back, too many of them, some good, some bad, all of them too real.

Sullivan soon fell asleep, but he slept fitfully. He had dreams, too many dreams, bad dreams, day-time nightmares. He was flooded with visions of all the people he had killed. There were Comanches, Comancheros, white bank robbers, and killers of various kinds.

He was chasing them and they were chasing him. He was catching them and they were catching him. He was shooting them and they were shooting him. He was scalping them and they were scalping him.

Suddenly he woke up! He was bouncing on the bed!

That dream was just too much, too much reality. He thought he had better stay awake and just rest.

Late in the afternoon, he got up, put his boots, hat, belt back on, and stuffed his Colt pistol back down in his belt. It was time to go meet the captain.

When he walked in the saloon, he found Captain Rice waiting on him at a table by one of the front windows, with his back to it. Rice stood up.

"Have a seat, Sullivan."

"Thanks."

A waitress walked up to them smiling.

"How may I help you Boys?"

"Steak, beans, bread, coffee," Rice said.

"Be right out, Boys."

As she walked away, Rice turned to Sullivan.

"When you get to Austin, give them all my regards. Major Pendergrass and I are old friends from way back."

"I will."

"Hope you'll have a safe trip."

"I intend to do just that."

When the meal was over, Sullivan went back to his room at the hotel. He went on to bed early. He had a long trip before him. But he had slept too much that afternoon.

He stayed awake a long time, staring at the ceiling. In a way he was glad. He never liked the nightmares.

Chapter 3

The next morning, Toombs Sullivan left Dallas, headed south toward Austin. He was glad to be returning to the place where he had begun as a Ranger. His route would take him right through the ranch owned by Josephine Wells, and then owned by Constance and her husband.

He thought about going around that property instead of going through it, avoiding any reminders of how things had been there. But no. He was a man. He could face it like he faced everything else in his life. A man faces whatever is before him. He could do it.

It was later on in the day, when he arrived at the ranch. He tied his horse at the water trough, pumping some water into it. He looked around some. Then he walked over to the house, opened the door, and went inside. With no one there, he decided to just spend the night. This would be his last chance to sleep in a bed for several days.

He went back outside, put his horse in the barn, took off his saddle, and took his gear and his rifles back to the house.

Everything there was very familiar and very strange, very welcoming and very distant, very warn and very cold. He felt at home and felt like a stranger. He wanted to stay and wanted to leave. He wanted to scream and he wanted to be silent. He wanted to sleep and knew he could not.

However, he was there. He had made that decision, and he would stand by it, spend the night, and be on the way the next day, putting that place behind him, hopefully forever.

Sleep did not come easily, and what there was of it was fleeting at best. He made it through the night, was fairly rested the next morning, and was ready to travel.

He had nearly two hundred miles to go. If he could make about fifty miles a day, he could be there in less than four days.

He knew that area well, where to stop for the night, where there was water, and where there was shelter in case bad weather came up.

On that day, the further south he went the more Indian sign he saw, unshod hoof prints from Indian ponies. He knew to be on the lookout, to be careful, and to keep a watchful eye. He never saw any fresh prints, nor did he ever see anything that made him think the Comanches were anywhere near him.

That evening, Sullivan stopped by a creek for the night. He watered his horse, made his camp, started a fire, and began cooking his meal of bacon, beans, and heating some bread he brought from the hotel kitchen.

Just before he began eating, he heard the sound of an approaching horse. He put down his plate, stood up, and pulled his pistol from his belt.

"Hello the camp!"

"Come on in."

The man got down off his horse and led it and another one near the camp where he tied them to a tree. He walked over to Sullivan.

Sullivan put his pistol back under his belt.

"Name's Buster Mize," he said, as he stuck out his hand.

"Toombs Sullivan."

They shook hands.

"I was just about to eat. Got plenty. You're welcomed to it."

"Why thank ya. I'm a little short on supplies myself. Headin' up to Dallas."

"Just came from there."

"Oh, good. How is the old girl?"

"Fine. Busy place. Ya know."

"Oh, yea. Love that place. First thing I'm gonna do is get a decent meal."

"You got your own plate? I only carry one with me."

"I got a plate."

Buster Mize walked over to his horse and pulled out of his saddle bag a plate, a fork, and a cup. He came back to the fire, took some of the food, and poured himself some coffee. He sat down by the fire and began eating, as did Sullivan.

"Goin' up to Dallas ya say?"

"Oh, yea. Got a cousin up there. Has a ranch out from town. Gonna work with him."

"Good. Fine horses you got there."

"My cousin raises horses. Sells a lot of'em."

The conversation continued for a while. Then both men turned in, weary from their journeys.

Sullivan went to sleep quickly, partly from the hard day and partly because he had not been sleeping well.

Late in the night, he was awakened by a noise. He rolled over and looked around. He saw Buster Mize taking his horse over toward his two. He grabbed his pistol, stood up, and spoke.

"Where ya goin' with my horse?"

Mize whirled around, pointing his pistol at Sullivan!

Sullivan fired!

Pow!

Buster Mize fell to the ground!

Sullivan walked over to him and kicked him to make sure he was dead.

"Raise horses, eh?"

He then took his horse back where it was and tied him to the tree.

The next morning, he buried Buster Mize, thew his pistol and rifle in the creek, threw his saddle over in some bushes, and set his horses free, chasing them off.

"Maybe you boys will find your way back to where you were or maybe some Comanche will give you a good home."

Four days later, he rode into Austin in the middle part of the day. He went immediately to the office of the Texas Rangers. There was a young man sitting at a desk in the outer office just inside the front door. He looked up.

"I'm Toombs Sullivan."

"Sullivan. Glad to meet you," he said, as he stood up and stuck out his hand. "We've been expecting you. I'm Johnny Tate, assistant to Major Pendergrass. You know the Major, I understand."

Sullivan shook his hand, as he said, "I do indeed. He swore me in years ago."

"He's waiting on you. Come on back."

Tate led Sullivan to the door of Major Henderson Pendergrass, Commander of the Texas Rangers. He knocked twice.

"Come!"

Johnny Tate opened the door.

"Here he is, Major."

"Come on in, Sullivan. So good to see you," he said, as he walked around his desk, and shook Sullivan's hand. "Have a seat."

As Sullivan took a chair, Major Pendergrass returned to his chair behind his desk.

"It's been a while. I remember so well when you started out here. You were a natural at rangering. I hated to see you leave here when we sent you north to Dallas, but they needed a good man there, and you were it. I got reports about you, of course, and you did mighty well. Then you left for a while, but I did not know anything about all that. Care to tell me?"

"Sure. I'll tell ya the whole story, Major."

Sullivan then related much of what he had done in the north as a Ranger, why he left for a while when he married Josephine Wells, and then why he had just come back. He hated telling about all of that because he had to relive it, but the Major needed to know what happened.

"My goodness, Son. You have certainly been through it. I'm sorry about all of that. One good thing, I guess, is that it all has brought you back to us. The men still remember you fondly."

"How are they, the ones I served with?"

"They're pretty well, I guess. Lost some, of course. Most the ones you rode with are scattered out all over the state. They got sent away the same way you did. Where there was a need we sent them, mostly one by one. We then kept hiring new ones to replace them for our companies here in Austin."

"So how are things down here, Major?"

"I'm afraid not much has changed. We're still fighting the Comanches. They rise up ever now and then, attack settlers and settlements. They'll burn out ranch homes, kill the people, steal their cattle and horses. We hear of it, and then send off a company or two to bring them to justice. Don't work most of the time. By the time we get to where the attack was, they are long gone. We bury the victims, follow the tracks as far as we can. Most of the time they'll break up that band, split up, usually after they have sold off the cattle. They divide up the horses. They love horses."

"It was and is still pretty much the same up north where I was. Think we will ever win this war we are fighting with them?"

"I don't know, but I have something else I need you to do other than fighting Indians. You have come back to us at just the right time, maybe just in time. Your experience and your knowledge of the land in the south make you the best man for this job."

"Don't keep me in suspense."

Chapter 4

"Sullivan, just how far south did you ever go?" Major Pendergrass asked.

Toombs Sullivan looked intently across the desk at Major Pendergrass. He had aged a little since he had seen him last, put on a few pounds, added a little gray around the temples, but not too much. Sullivan had aged himself with what he had been through, so he understood the march of time.

"I been down below Corpus Christi. You remember that gang of cut-throats, Comanches, Mexicans, Breeds, and Whites we went after."

"I do indeed. Nasty business, their kind. I got something further south I need you to take on. Though you are not a Captain yet, I want you to take Company L. Their Captain died of some illness a few weeks back. William Boyd is in that company."

"I remember him well."

"He'll be second to you. Though not a sergeant yet, he's been sort of in change of them since they have had no leader these few weeks, but they have not gone out anywhere, just restin' up, so to speak. But they're ready now."

"Okay, what is it?"

"We got a bunch of cattle thieves down along the border, down around Brownsville.

What do you know about Brownsville?"

"Not a thing."

"It was founded in eighteen and forty-eight by a man named Charles Stillman. He named it after Fort Brown which was named after a Major Jacob Brown who was killed in the war with Mexico. Friend maybe or something. I don't know. Don't matter. And the Battle of Brownsville, some call it the Battle of Palmito Ranch, was said to be the last battle of the Civil War. Others say the last battle was at West Point, Georgia. I don't know. Don't matter. Brownsville is where our people smuggled in cotton, got it over into Mexico, so it could then be shipped to England, Europe.

"Well, there's some Mexican cattle thieves crossing over into Texas, stealing cattle, taking it over into Mexico, and then they kill'em, scrape the tallow from the skins, and ship it to Cuba. Big market for them. They leave the rest to rot in the sun. Just leave the meat, hides, and all.

"They are led by a man by the name of Fernando De La Cruz Antonia De Vega. He was a young officer at the Alamo. He was a favorite of Santa Ana. He became a general eventually. Guess maybe he retired or something. Anyway, he found something more lucrative than being in the army. He's got an army of sorts around him now, some say maybe fifty men or more. Some say it's a hundred."

"Who are they hitting?"

"There's a big rancher down there, Horace Charles Roland. His ranch is the Rolling R. Their brand on their cattle is two Rs. He began that ranch back in eighteen and fifty-three. He had been a steamboat captain under General Zachery Taylor. After the war with Mexico, he hauled goods up the Rio Grand.

"Well, one day he decided to attend a big fair up at Corpus Christi. So, he rode from Brownsville all the way up on horseback. He had never before seen all that country. He fell in love with it. He had a lot of money. He bought over eight hundred thousand acres of it. They say he has about eighty thousand head of cattle. That's a lot of beef. He sold the Confederacy that much and more.

"There's a story in the Bible about a man having a hundred sheep. One of them gets lost. He leaves the others to go out and find that one.

"Captain Roland has been in touch with me by letter. He sometimes will let the Indians take a few, if they are in bad need. But even a man with eighty thousand head don't want even one stolen and carried away to Mexico."

"Why don't he go after them himself?"

"He's tried, I understand. But it's an army he's facing down there."

"You want me and one company of Rangers to go face an army? An army he can't face himself with all his men, and he must have a large group of drovers."

"And they are just that – drovers. They ain't soldiers or lawmen."

"You told him you'd send the Rangers down there?"

"I did."

"Well at least give me two companies instead of just one."

"Uh, all right. Tell ya what. Company J will go along. They've just come in from being out a couple of weeks. They need to rest up a little. Captain John Maine will go with you. You'll be co-leaders, but the mission is yours since you know more about that country than he does. That don't mean a Sergeant gives orders to a Captain, but he'll follow your uh, council, shall we say."

"That's better, but it's still twenty-four or five against maybe a hundred."

"Or maybe fifty, Sullivan."

"Or maybe two hundred."

"Just do your best."

"If I don't, Major, I'll be dead."

"Take a few days to get ready. Get to know the men as best you can. Get with Captain Maine. I'll let him know this is your baby. I reserved a room for ya at the hotel."

"Thanks. You been around babies much, Major?"

"Well, no."

"They do unexpected things when you are least prepared for them."

"All right. It's not your baby. It's your mission."

"Thanks. That sounds better."

"I'll see you again before you leave."

"Sure, Major. It's good to be with you again."

"Glad to have ya."

Sullivan got up, shook the Major's hand, and left.

He walked out of the office and went across the street to a saloon he had visited many times when he was stationed in Austin before. He took a seat at a table.

Then he saw a young lady he had known back then. It was Lydia Langley. When she spotted him, she walked over to his table.

"Well, well. You're Toombs Sullivan."

"Always have been."

"I remember you."

"I remember you as well, Lydia."

"Indeed you do. I heard they had sent you up to Dallas. That was a couple of days after you left. You didn't even come tell me goodbye."

"Didn't have time. But I have come back to tell you hello."

"I'm glad you have. I see you lived through whatever it was you was doin'."

"I did. I am living proof."

"What can I get for you?"

"The usual. Steak and what goes with it. And coffee. And whiskey first."

"Sure thing."

Lydia came back with a glass and a whiskey bottle.

"This is on me."

"Thanks, Lydia."

She poured him a drink.

"Your food will be out soon."

"No hurry. No worry. I got nothin' else to do but sit here."

Fifteen minutes later, she came back with his food and the coffee.

"Hope you enjoy."

"I will."

"What ya doing tonight? Late tonight."

"Sleeping."

She smiled and walked away.

Lydia Langley was an attractive woman. He always liked her. Still did. But Toombs Sullivan had no intention of getting involved with her or any other woman. He had nothing but bad luck with the women in his life. He needed to concentrate on cows.

Chapter 5

Sullivan left the saloon, and went down the street to the hotel where he had stayed when he was stationed in Austin before. He knew it would feel like home, and after all, it was the official unofficial home of the Rangers in the city. It was also the place where he had some unpleasant memories. It was there in that hotel where he found Captain Springtown and Ned Crawford butchered by the breed Pledger. But there were many unpleasant memories in many places. He could not hide or run from any of them. He understood that. The Major had told him his room was already reserved for him.

Sullivan led his horse down the street to the stables where all the Rangers kept theirs.

He said to the owner of the stables, "I'm a Ranger. I'll settle my account with you in a day or two. That all right?"

"Sure. All you Rangers are good for it. Say, I remember you from a few years back. You gonna be here now?"

"Yep. Been up Dallas way and Fort Worth. Back here for good now. I think. If the Indians don't take my hair and the best of me."

"Let's hope they don't. Put'im down there on the right. Little beyond half-way."

"Thanks."

When he got the horse in the stall, he took off the saddle, putting it over the wall. Then he picked up his saddle bags, a large travel bag and his two rifles, the Sharps over his shoulder with a strap and his Winchester in his left hand.

"Name?"

"Toombs Sullivan."

"You look loaded down there," the man said, as Sullivan was leaving.

"I'll make it. Ain't the first time."

"Have a good day."

"I'm having one. You too."

Sullivan walked in the door of the hotel, stepping over to the front desk.

"Hey, I'm Sullivan. I have a room here. Reserved."

"Oh, yes, Mister Sullivan. Room two-thirteen upstairs."

"Thanks," Sullivan said, as he took the key from the clerk's hand.

He turned around, and looked across the large parlor area where he saw a familiar person walking toward him.

"Sullivan! How are you?"

"Fine, Boyd. How about yourself?"

"Oh, I'm doing well, all things considered. Mighty glad to have you back down here where you belong."

"Let me put my things in my room. Then we'll go across the street. I'll buy you a steak. I just ate a while ago, but I could use another drink."

"Sounds great. I love steak."

"Ever the poet. I'll be right back."

Sullivan climbed the stairs, turned left and went down the hall to his room, thinking all the while of two-thirteen. If it was on the first floor, would it be just plain thirteen or one-thirteen. Why thirteen? I don't need any help finding bad luck. I can do that on my own.

He opened the door, went inside, placed his saddle bags on the bed, his travel bag on a table, and his two rifles in a corner just to the right of the bed. He looked around. It all looked the same as it had several years ago. Nothing had changed at all.

When he went back downstairs, he found William Boyd standing by the door waiting on him.

"Same old hang-out over there," he said to Boyd.

"Yeah, still the same. The whiskey is still fine and the food still ain't half bad."

"Yeah, I found out. Let's go."

They went across the street and entered the saloon, taking a table off to the right beside the window so they could look out.

The young waitress came over to their table in a couple of minutes.

"Hi, Willie," she said, with a big smile. "Who is your friend here?"

"This is Toombs Sullivan, one of us. He's back here now after being up at Dallas a few years. Toombs, this is Katie Welch."

"Nice to meet ya," Sullivan said. "Are you Welsh?"

"No. Just a girl from Mississippi."

"What brought you out here?"

"What brings all of us out here?"

"I understand. How about a steak for my friend here, potatoes, bread, coffee, whiskey."

"Won't be long," she replied. "You were in here earlier. Saw you talking to Lydia."

"Yep. Known her a few years. I was stationed here before. Back now."

"So she tells me," she remarked, as she walked away.

Turning to Boyd, Sullivan asked, "Did the Major brief you on what we'll be doing?"

"He briefed me briefly. Not much to go on. Just go down there and stop them. Sounds simple enough."

"I guess that depends on how many of them there are. Could be fifty, could be a hundred, he seemed to think. He's givin' us Company J."

"Even if there are only fifty, we'll be two companies against twice our number. If a hundred, well, I don't know."

"Yeah. Lookin' on the bright side of things, we have chased after a large number of Comanches a number of times."

"Yeah, Sullivan, and the problem was we caught up with them."

"Speaking of them, any trouble with any of those Comanches lately."

"Always trouble with them. We'll have to watch out for them and the bad men we are goin' after, both at the same time. This ain't goin' to be an easy job he's givin' us. They're all after the same cattle, the Comanches and them Mexican rustlers."

"If it was easy, he wouldn't have chosen us."

"By the time we get through here, all the men should be back at the hotel. I'll introduce you to them, get them all together."

Soon the food and coffee and whiskey arrived.

"Anything else, Men?"

"No. This is it," Sullivan said.

"If ya need anything, let me know."

"Sure."

As Katie Welch walked away, Boyd said, "Let's eat. Bless Pete."

Sullivan poured himself a small glass of whiskey and drank it down.

"Understand you been through some hard times. Again."

"Yep. Are there no secrets anymore?"

"Word gets around. We been keepin' up with you. Hard to lose a woman. Twice."

"You ever married, Boyd? Don't think I ever asked you about that."

"I was. Twice also. It was before the war. The first time was a fine girl. Name of Susan. Susan Logan. Before I was a Ranger. We was trying to raise cattle on a little place. I come into town to get supplies. Got back late in the day. I found her in the barn. What was left of her. Comanches got her. It was a small band of'em. I buried her and chased them down. Did worse to them than they done to her. Well, anyway. The second gal I married was Ruth Ann Clemons. She weren't no fine girl. But I didn't know it. She run off with a drunk cowboy. They didn't get far. I kill him outright. Took her on down to Galveston, put her on a boat, and sent her back to New Orleans where she was from. I came back home and sold the place. I joined the Rangers because I had the taste of Indian blood in my mouth. The war broke out, and I quit the Rangers, unlike so many of the boys. I joined the army to go kill Yankees because that scoundrel who took Ruth Ann away was from Indiana. I must've killed him a dozen times in the war. Well, I came back here, and been a Ranger ever since."

"I had no idea you been through all that."

"All of us have secrets, things that happened to us, and we can't tell nobody and don't want to because it don't do no good, and who wants to live through it again and again. Some of these young Rangers ain't been through much yet. Some have, or they wouldn't be Rangers. Others, the older ones, are Rangers for a reason. And the reasons ain't very clean and nice."

"I guess you're right."

"You'll like the boys."

Chapter 6

When Sullivan and Boyd returned to the hotel, they found the men waiting on them.

They were gathered in the spacious parlor. Boyd spoke first.

William Boyd was a veteran Ranger. He stood just under six feet tall, stocky build, fair complexion, reddish hair. He had blue-green eyes and a thick mustache, and kept his hair cut short and close on the sides of his head.

"Men, this is Sergeant Toombs Sullivan. He's going to lead us when we go out in a day or two."

"Thanks, Boyd. Well, I used to be stationed here, but was sent up to Dallas for a few

years. It's a long story, most of them are, and I won't bore you with it. How about ya tell me yore name and a little something about you? I know Boyd here already. We were together when I first joined the Rangers."

The Rangers all looked around the room to see who would go first. Then one of them sitting closest to Sullivan began.

"Ben Warner. Grew up here in Texas. Joined the Rangers just after the war. I came home, and found my parents buried in the ground and the home place burned out. No doubt who did it. I been gettin' even ever since." Ben Warner was long and tall, dark tan except for his forehead which was pale looking. He wore the usual Texas Ranger garb, large kerchief around his neck, a blue shirt, brown pants tucked into high boots, a vest, gun belt high on his waste. His waste-coat was across his knee. He held his large hat in his left hand.

"I'm Johnny Hunt. Came to Texas with a friend when the war was over. I had nothin' left in Tennessee. My friend was killed by Comanches the first week we were here. I managed to get away from them, but I been lookin' for'em ever since." He was medium, height, stocky, and red-faced. He dressed very much like Warner.

In fact, as Sullivan looked around the room, he could see they were all dressed like Boyd, Warner, and Hunt. And they were dressed like he was also.

"Uh, Jack Stamps. From right here in Texas. Fought in the war. I knew about the Rangers all my life. And I always wanted to be one. So, here I am. Fought in the war first though, like most of us here, I guess. Made it home alive. Thank the good God." He had a dark complexion, black hair, dark eyes. He was tall and muscular.

"Billy Smith. I had been in the Rangers about two years before the war. So I was not put in the Army. Those of us in the Rangers were kept here to try to contain the Comanches." He was fair in the face, with blond hair, not tall, not stout, just average looking.

"Ludie Lancaster here. From New Orleans. I was at Vicksburg that whole time. I done been to hell. Fighting Indians is no worse than that. My aim and goal in life is to kill them before they kill me. Period." Ludie was tall, thin, wiry looking. Dark complexion.

"I'm Buck Stansel, one of them Rangers that stayed here during the war. That's all." He was soft-spoken, reserved looking, average build and height, brown hair and eyes.

"Wayne Wainwright. Why my folks gave me the name of Wayne, I got no idea. Makes me sound like I am stuttering or something, which I ain't. Been a Ranger a long time. Can't hardly remember when I was not one. Missed the war. Much to my regret. These boys like to call me Wayne Wayne." He had sandy curly hair, bright blue eyes that drew you in, a ready smile, large white teeth. Average size and build.

"Tommy Jackson here. No distinguishing marks or history about me. I am new, and I am the youngest. I never killed anybody. Went into the war toward the end. They made me a doctor's aide, knew nothing about medicine, still don't. I was fifteen." His looks were those of a still teenage young man. He was innocent looking, almost immature looking, blond, blue eyes.

"Jackson Summers. I ask everybody to call me Jackson so every time somebody calls out for Jack Stamps over there, I won't think they want me, but they won't do it. They just aggravate me for the fun of it," he said with a smile. He was shorter than most, but strong looking, had black hair, cut close on the sides, and bushy eyebrows.

"My name is Ben Long, and that's the long and the short of it. Though my name is Long, I ain't because I'm short. But I don't care. Fought in the war, where I grew up, but did not grow up, if ya know what I mean." He was indeed the shortest of the men. He was bright looking, had a dark mustache, and was very thin.

"Buck Johnson. I was in the war, been a cattle drover, buffalo hunter, scout, and all around no good for much, but 'cept I love bein' a Ranger best of all." His looks seemed to verify his own description of himself. He was thin looking, had rather long hair, a mustache that curled around his mouth with a little patch of hair under his lower lip.

"All right, thanks men," Sullivan said. "Well, I came to Texas after the war. I grew up in Georgia, but had nothing to keep me there. I wanted to see the country. Maybe have some adventure. Find my own way. I sort'a fell into being a Ranger accidently when I saved a Major's life in east Texas in a saloon. He invited me to join up. I had nothing better to do. I fought Indians south of here a lot, went to Dallas for a few years, fought them there and robbers of various kinds, became a town deputy in Fort Worth, but decided the Rangers is where I belong. I have seen the country, and have had more adventures than I care to remember, just like most of you. But here we are. We got a job to do. I think you have been told about it already. So we'll go down south as far as we can and try to clean up that mess down there.

"Now, you got a problem, a question, a concern, you come to me with it. I am just one of you, that's all. If I can't solve it, answer it, fix it, we'll see if we can find a way. I'll depend on you, and you can depend on me.

"We'll pull out of here in a day or two, so get yore gear ready, and yore weapons in good shape, and your horse.

"When we leave here, we'll go down to San Antonio and spend the night. Then we head south-east. I hope we don't run into Comanches, but we very well could. Nobody goes anywhere alone except whoever is ridin' point for us. Everybody gets to stand guard at night. We're takin' some food. But we'll probably need to kill some game along the way.

"Questions anyone?"

"I got a question," said Tommy Jackson.

"All right."

"How long you think we might be gone?"

"Ha ha ha," some of the men laughed.

"Tommy has a girlfriend over at the saloon. His first," said Jackson Summers. "He don't want to leave her. He's afraid she'll be gone or have another boyfriend when we get back."

Tommy looked embarrassed as his face reddened.

"A good question, Tommy. It's Tommy, right?"

Tommy nodded his head slightly and half-way smiled.

"Don't really know. Several weeks I'd say. Not days, months, or years. We don't know what we'll get into, what the place will be like. But I can tell ya this much. It ain't gonna be quick and it ain't gonna be easy. You can go see that girl tonight and tell her that. Beyond what I said, I got no idea.

"Anything else?

"All right. Get yore stuff ready. Get you ready. Eat good, rest well, and we'll do the best we can.

"That's all."

Chapter 7

Captain John Maine was in charge of Company J. He was the typical long tall Texan who had been in the Rangers for almost twenty years. He was forty-five years old. He had been married once, but his wife had died of consumption. He was almost boney faced, had a deep tan, the wrap-around mustache, brown hair with a little white slipping in. He wore high boots, black pants tucked in, a white shirt, and instead of a vest or a waste-coat, he wore a dark gray coat that looked like it had been part of a suit. A blue kerchief was around his neck fitting loosely. He wore a big black hat. He was not a happy looking man, was somewhat bitter, hardened by events, fights he had been in, Indians he had chased and killed, and had been chased by some who wanted to kill him.

John Maine was waiting in the parlor when Sullivan came down the stairs.

"You Sullivan?"

"I am."

"John Mane," he said, as he walked toward Sullivan, his right hand extended.

"Pleased to meet ya."

"Likewise. I'll buy ya breakfast for ya. Come on."

They walked into the hotel dining room. Other Rangers were already there eating. They sat at a table that was to one side in a corner. The room was filled with various sounds, cups hitting saucers, forks on plates, conversations, laughter. There was the aroma of coffee, bacon, cigar smoke all mixed together. A waitress saw them and came right over.

"What'a ya have?" the young waitress asked.

Looking at Sullivan for approval, Maine replied, "Eggs, bacon, bread, grits, butter, jam, coffee and lots of it quick."

Sullivan smiled, and said, "Yep. Good."

"Small talk later. How ya wanna go about the business we have at hand? How ya wanna get down there?"

"Been thinking about that. I been out with two companies before. Sometime we were together. Sometime we split up, but kept in touch. I'm sure your experience has been the same. You been at this longer than I have. But what about this? What say we stick pretty close together until we get to San Antonio? Spend the night there. Then from there on down, we split apart, say about a mile or so, no more. We'll be in Comanche territory. Course, they are everywhere anyway, but seem to have strongholds more often down there. That way we all don't get attacked at once, but if there is trouble, then gunshots will bring the other of us to the rescue. We stay in touch all the way with riders between us pretty often. We don't camp at night together, but stay apart. How's that sound?"

"Sounds good to me. Well, Sir, you got a good company there."

"Looks like it. Only one man with not much experience, I think. He's young, but we all were. He'll learn quickly, of necessity. Tell me about yores."

"They're a good bunch. We been together for some time. We know how each other thinks and works, and seem to mesh together pretty well."

In a few minutes, two waitresses brought out their food and coffee.

"Here ya go, Boys. Hope ya enjoy. If ya need anything, let me know."

"Thanks," they both said at the same time.

They began eating, and did not speak for a brief time.

"Leave out tomorrow?" Maine asked.

"Good."

"Gotta get supplies together and horses ready."

"Uh-huh."

"I'll get the men on it."

"Yep, me too."

During the meal, they talked about a variety of subjects. Maine wanted to know about Sullivan's experience in the war. He told him briefly where he had been and what he had done and seen, but really did not want to get into all that very much, feeling that many things are better left where they are, buried some place in the past.

Also, Sullivan did not want to talk about his two wives and what had happened to them. All of that was better left unsaid as well. For that reason, he did not ask Maine about his past. He was a long-time Ranger and a good leader. That was enough, and was all Sullivan needed to know.

When they had finished their meal, Sullivan thanked Maine for his hospitality. Then they went their separate ways, each of them having a lot to do to be ready for the next day's trip.

As they were leaving the dining room, William Boyd came up to Sullivan.

"Sarge, I told the boys to start getting everything together, and sent several to go buy all the supplies we'll need."

"Good. Uh, you can call me Toombs or Sullivan if ya like. Ya don't have to use the title. It's a little stuffy, and I never got used to it. It's like when somebody calls me Mister Sullivan. I turn around to see if my father is standing there. He ain't. I sometime don't know who Sergeant Sullivan is."

"Sure," Boyd replied with a smile.

"Well, Boyd, tomorrow is the day."

"Yes, it is."

"How ya think the boys will do?"

"They'll be fine."

"Any weak spots?"

"No. Only the young one, Tommy. We'll need to watch him to see if he'll be all right. I expect he will."

"Who's our two best men, in case something happens to us on the way or after we get there?"

"I'd say Ben Warner and Johnny Hunt. Both of them could take charge if need be. They got good experience, and are pretty level headed. The other boys seem to like them and respect them."

"Good. Let's hope they won't be needed to do that, but we never know when we go out."

"Right. Anything else?"

"Guess not," answered Sullivan.

"I'll go see how the supplies are comin' along."

"Thanks, Boyd."

Chapter 8

The next morning, the two Texas Ranger companies pulled out of Austin not long after eight o'clock. They were a formidable sight as they came down the main street in columns of two with company L first and then Company J behind them. Sullivan and Maine were out front riding side by side. Each company had two pack mules loaded down with supplies of food, extra ammo, cooking pots, medical supplies, and any and everything they might need and could remember to bring along.

Several people along the sidewalks on both sides of the street saw them, knew who they were, and basically where they were going and why. Some waved, some spoke, and some offered encouragement. There was hardly anyone who did not stop and look at them, knowing some of them might not ever come back. It was a solemn moment.

The Rangers felt that as well. All of them had gone out on journeys like this one when not all of them came back. But they were used to that in a way, if you can ever get used to dying, seeing death, tasting death, smelling death. They had to learn how to accept it, bury their friends where they lay, and get on with whatever it was they went out to accomplish. It was a part of the job. If they could not accept that, then they could go herd cows somewhere. There were always plenty of cows.

About a mile out of town, Sullivan looked back at William Boyd, who was right behind him, and said, "Boyd, take the point."

"Sure," he responded, as he rode on by Sullivan and Maine and sped out ahead of the two columns of Rangers.

Less than an hour later, Boyd came rushing back to make a report.

"We got trouble up ahead. I saw a lot of unshod pony tracks. Comanche no doubt."

"How many you think?" asked Maine.

"Hard to say, Cap'n. A good many. I'd guess, oh, I don't know, maybe twenty, thirty, or more."

"You couldn't tell what they were up to? No cattle tracks?"

"None that I could see. Must be a hunting party of some kind."

"Trying to see what they can get into, I guess," said Sullivan. "Looking for some victims."

"What do you want to do?" asked Maine.

"Well, we didn't come down this way to fight Indians. We got a bigger job ahead of us. But we can't ignore them if they show themselves. We can try to avoid them if possible, but if they confront us, we'll have to take them on."

"I agree," Maine replied.

"All right, Boyd, go on back out and keep us informed about where they are."

"Right."

As Boyd rode away, Sullivan and Maine looked at each other with expressions that said this is all we need, though neither of them said a word.

Sullivan waved his hand forward and the Rangers moved out.

It was only about eighty or ninety miles from Austin to San Antonio. The Rangers could easily make that trip in two days, having to spend the night out only once. They were used to camping out in the open country. It was part of the job. But they always looked forward to hotels in places like San Antonio where they could have a roof over their heads and some good food.

A couple of hours later, Boyd came back to make another report.

"Captain, Sergeant, them Indians cut off toward the west, so we won't be following them anymore."

"Good, and thanks," Sullivan replied.

Boyd turned his horse around as he rode on ahead.

Toward the end of the day, Boyd came riding back toward the two companies.

"There's a good place to camp for the night on the San Marcos River down not far from the town of San Marcos," he reported. "We'll be there soon."

Sullivan looked over at Maine, who replied, "We better camp there, and not go into town looking for rooms. Better save our money, since we'll be spending some in San Antonia tomorrow night."

Sullivan nodded his head, and said to Boyd, "Take us there."

Thirty-five minutes later, they were setting up camp by the river. First, the horses and mules were allowed to drink from the river, and the men did as well. Saddles were taken off the horses, and the horses were tied out near the camp, maybe thirty or forty yards away. Then the packs were removed from the mules, and they were tied out by the horses. Several fires were built. Some of the men began cooking bacon, heating some bread, opening cans of beans and putting the contents in pots hung over the fires. Coffee was soon boiling. Each man carried his own plate, cup, utensils. Two portable folding tables were set up.

Once the food and coffee were ready, the pots and pans were set on the tables. The men filed past, dipping the food and pouring coffee for themselves. Then they sat down to eat, some on the ground, some on fallen trees and stumps, a couple of them on large boulders. When the meal was finished, everything that had been used was washed in the river. The left-over food was thrown in the water so it would flow on down away from the camp. No sense inviting any wild animal to come in the camp looking for it. There was not much left anyway. The Rangers tended to eat everything in sight.

A schedule for guard duty was set up with two-hour shifts. From Company L Ben Warner would take the first watch. From Company J Jimmy Crabtree would also be on duty. One of them on one end of the remuda, the other on the other end nearest the river.

It was Jimmy Crabtree by the river this first watch.

Near the end of that first watch, Crabtree heard a commotion of some sort. He realized Warner was in trouble. He raced toward him. Even though it was pitch-black dark, he could make out two figures, one on the ground, the other on top of him with a tomahawk raised in the air. He wasted no time, firing one shot from his Winchester. The Indian fell across Warner's faced.

From under the Comanche, Warner was able to mumble, "Thanks."

With that shot, the camp was alerted. All of the Rangers came running with guns drawn.

By the time they got there, Warner was on his feet, the Indian lying near him. They all looked at the Comanche.

"They love horses," Johnny Hunt said.

"And this one ain't alone," replied Sullivan.

"We better double the guard," Maine said. "And keep a watchful eye out."

Two more guards were placed around the camp. It was Buck Stansel and Young John West from Company J.

However, it may as well have been everybody else as well. Though the rest of them laid back down, no one could sleep with the knowledge that the Comanches knew where they were and how many horses they had and where the horses were.

Though a few of them managed to doze off a little now and then, most of them laid on the ground with their eyes wide open staring at the stars.

They rotated the guard duty every two hours as planned. Each man standing guard heard sounds in the night, not just the usual sounds, but also other sounds either real or imagined.

Sullivan was no different from all of the others. His eyes never closed. He could never relax. Every once in a while, he got up and walked around checking on the men.

"Hear anything?"

"Yes."

"What?"

"I don't know."

"See anything?"

"No. Not really. Only ghosts and bugger bears."

"They won't hurt. Much."

"Thanks."

Chapter 9

Late the next afternoon, they arrived in San Antonio. They put the horses and mules in a livery stable, taking their personal items with them, and leaving their supplies in the care of the stable owner. They had done business with him many times, and knew he could be trusted to keep an eye on what was theirs. They paid him well to do that.

Then they went to one of the hotels and checked in.

Later, they ate a meal in the hotel dining room. After that, most of them went to one of the several saloons. A few sat around the hotel parlor. Luckily it was an uneventful evening, one they needed.

The next morning, they headed south-west out of town toward an uncertain time. It was nearly three hundred miles to their destination. That was about five or six days in wild country where anything could happen.

Captain Maine took Company J and cut across east away from Company L. They would be about a mile away as both companies headed toward the south-east.

"Johnny Hunt!" called Sullivan. "Take the point!"

Hunt galloped on past Sullivan, leaving the company in the dust.

They were making good time for about two hours, when suddenly they began hearing gunfire from the east!

Bang!

Bang!

Pow!

Bang!

Pow!

Pow!

The column came to a sudden stop as they all looked in that direction.

They could hardly believe what they were hearing. It was too early for any big encounter with Comanches! They were thinking that maybe further down they would have trouble. But not today!

The Rangers looked to the east.

They looked at Sullivan.

Sullivan looked from the east back at them.

Then he shouted at them.

"Let's go!"

They all broke ranks as they raced off to try and help Company J.

Could they get there in time?

Who were they facing?

Was it a few Indians? Was it a large band of them? A war party? Did they stumble into a village? A camp? Their point man would have prevented that.

Could they get there in time?

Could they get there in time?

Could they get there in time?

All these questions and more tumbled together in their heads as they tried to make sense of something they knew nothing about.

Minutes later, the gunfire was louder. Dust was rising in the air just ahead over a ridge.

They were closer now.

Hurry! Hurry!

When they topped the ridge, they saw what looked like thirty or forty Comanches surrounding the Rangers of Company J.

"Open fire!" Sullivan shouted.

They rode as fast as they could toward the Comanches.

When the Comanches saw them, they began firing back at Company L. Then suddenly they left, riding off toward the south.

"Do we go after them?" William Boyd asked.

"No." Sullivan answered. "They could be wanting to lure us into a trap where there's even more of them. Let'em go. We'll deal with them later. Let's see about the men here."

As they approached Company J, it looked like half of them were dead from the surprise attack.

Sullivan and his men dismounted.

"Glad to see you Boys," said Sergeant Sam Bickers. "They about got the best of us. Guess they did get the best of us."

Bickers looked around at the ground.

"We got six dead, including Captain Maine. That don't leave but six of us now."

"Guess you're in charge now. You're Bickers, right."

"Yeah."

"Y'all are now a part of our company. All right, Boys," Sullivan said matter-of-factly, "let's get'em, in the ground."

The men pulled shovels off the pack-mules and began digging the hard dirt. Two hours later, six holes in the ground became graves for the six dead Rangers. They picked the dead men up and carried them over to the graves. They took off their boots and their gun-belts. They gently placed each man in a grave. They folded their hands over their chests. Then they placed their hats over their faces so the dust would not get in the eyes and mouths and noses. They covered them over with dirt. They made six grave markers, looking like crosses as best as they get them to look that way.

Then they all stood around the graves with their hats in their hands, a solemn look on each face.

Sergeant Bickers read the Twenty-third Psalm.

Sullivan said a prayer.

"God in Heaven, these men died here today. We weren't expectin' this. Nobody was. They weren't. I don't know if they was ready, but I hope they all was. Ready or not, we're sendin' them to you. Do what you can for them. Help their families if they got any.

Christ sake. Amen."

He paused a minute, and then said, "Boys, this just goes to show ya how fragile life is and how long it don't last. This could'a been any one of the rest of us. The fact that we are standing here instead of bein' where they are is just fate or luck or the good God lookin' out for us for reasons we don't know and can't never understand. Let it be a lesson for us all."

Then he said, "We need to have a meeting, Boys. Follow me."

They walked over to the horses and gathered in a semi-circle around Sullivan.

"Here it is, plain and simple. We didn't none of us come down here to fight Indians.

We come down here with a mission to stop Mexican cattle thieves. We knew we might run into Comanches, but we never expected this. But this changes things, at least for me. I say we ain't gonna let this pass and go unpunished. I say we go get these savages and do to them what's been done here today. We do that first. We get them cattle thieves later, if we live long enough to do it. What say you?"

"We're with you, Sullivan," answered Bickers.

Sullivan looked into the eyes of each man standing there. There were nods, a few said yep.

"All right, then. Let's go get it done. Boyd, take the point. Uh, Bickers what happened to yore point man?"

"It was young John West. He never came back. Ain't no tellin'. If the Comanch got him, that'd be seven."

Sullivan nodded his head, and said, "Let's go."

The men walked over to their horses. Sullivan spoke again.

"I don't guess I need to remind ya, but I will anyway. Check yore weapons, pistols and rifles. Be sure you are loaded up. And be sure you got more ammo at yore quick disposal. When we catch up with'em we ain't gonna have time to be lookin' for ammo. I want us to be gettin' rid of it as fast as we can."

Chapter 10

As William Boyd rode off, following the tracks of the Indian ponies, Sullivan and the Rangers mounted up.

Company L was now made up of twenty men instead of thirteen, but there was no longer another company with them. Whatever they did was now going to be different from what Sullivan had imagined. Twenty men in one company instead of twenty-six men in two companies might become a problem. But this was not the first time Sullivan had faced a problem. Solving a problem and pressing on was what the Texas Rangers did. It was just part of the job. Be a man and face it. That was it.

As they rode off following Wiliam Boyd, they saw a lone rider approaching them. He was about a hundred yards away. They stopped, and Sullivan said to Bickers, who was beside him, "Is that yore man?"

"Yep. That's Young John West."

In moments, West pulled up his horse in front of them.

"What happened to you?" Bickers asked.

Looking surprised, West replied, "I been out ahead looking for the best way, down south-east, but I thought I could hear the faintest sound of gun-fire. What happened to you all?"

"Ain't but six of us left now. So we joined up with Sullivan and his men. They're all dead. The captain too."

"My God. What happened?"

"A right large bunch of Comanches jumped us. Before we knew what happened, they was on us. Killed six of us right quick. Did you never see them, sign, nothing?"

"Naw. I was careful to look for sign, but never saw nothin'. What now?"

"We goin' after'em," Bickers answered.

"We're gonna kill every one of them," Sullivan added. Then he said, "Let's go men."

The Rangers followed the tracks of Boyd and all the tracks of the unshod Indian ponies. The tracks were easy to follow.

In the late evening, they saw Boyd approaching them. They stopped to wait on him.

When he came to them, he gave his report.

"There's a good place to camp for the night up ahead. It's along a creek. Good water. Looks to me like the Comanches are on down the creek. Runs off to the south-west. Don't know how far they are, but I'm willin' to bet my pistol they're camped there somewhere."

"All right, Boyd, lead us on down there," answered Sullivan.

A few miles further, and they were at the creek. They went about setting up the camp, watering the horses and mules, gathering wood for fires, unpacking the mules, and tying off the animals.

After preparing food and eating it, Sullivan asked Bickers to post guards and set them up for the night in two-hour shifts.

Once that was done, the men began to settle in for the night. They spread their bed-rolls, cleaned their weapons, and talked quietly among themselves about the events of the day.

Sullivan got Boyd's attention and motioned him over to him.

"Get yore rifle. Let's take a walk down the creek a ways. If they are camped along this creek, then they can't be far away. I want to know where they are. I don't want any surprises tonight or early in the morning."

They both got their rifles, chambered a round, and began moving along the edge of the creek.

They approached Wayne Wainwright, who was taking the first watch, standing by the creek.

"We're taking a walk," Sullivan said. "Don't shoot us when we come back. And tell yore replacement where we are. And the pass-word is Sam Houston. Tell him."

"I will. Be careful."

The two Rangers slipped away into the shadows of the trees along the banks of the creek. They moved quietly, deliberately, slowly so as not to cause any noise or disturb the night birds and creatures.

They knew the Indians would have their guards out just as they did. They did not want to stumble into their camp or near their guards.

The slow pace made the journey seem even longer than it was, but this was no time to be careless. Caution was the watch-word for them.

After close to an hour, they came to a place where they could see camp-fires flickering in the darkness. Sullivan looked around at Boyd, pointed his finger to his eyes, and then pointed to the lights. Boyd nodded his head.

They could hear the Comanches talking, laughing, and seeming to celebrate something.

Sullivan knew they were celebrating having killed some white men. He was incensed by that. Sweet revenge is what he wanted.

They stood there for several minutes, not moving, not whispering, not making any noise.

Then they heard rustling in the leaves on the ground and the weeds. They held their breath.

The Comanche stepped over to the creek, cleared his throat, and then began peeing in the water. He was only twenty yards away. Sullivan and Boyd almost laughed, but managed to control themselves.

When the Comanche left and walked back down the creek toward his camp, Sullivan and Boyd slipped back up the creek. The journey was quicker this time. Soon they came to Wainwright, who was still on guard.

"Who is it?" Wainwright asked.

"Sam Houston," Sullivan replied.

"Come on in. . . . What did ya find?"

"Indians."

"Is that good or bad?"

"It better be good for us and bad for them. We'll find out, maybe in the morning."

It would be another sleepless or mostly sleepless night for Sullivan. They knew now where the Indians were. What if one or some of them did what he and Boyd did. They would be discovered in the night. He knew he better be on the alert in spite of having guards out. He laid down by the fire, watched the flickering shadows, and listened out for unusual noises. Some hours before dawn he drifted away.

Chapter 11

"We'll ride part of the way to where they 're camped. When we get close, we'll dismount, lead our horses in. If they're still there, we'll mount up, and charge in on'em."

The Rangers got on their horses. They rode slowly along beside the creek. When they drew near, Sullivan pointed at Boyd. He then signaled that the Rangers should dismount and begin walking.

Boyd gave Sullivan the reins to his horse, as he moved on ahead of the company. He eased along by the creek, careful to not make any noise, just like the night before. He soon disappeared from the view of the company.

Sullivan turned to the other Rangers. "Get your pistols ready. We'll ride in on them. Catch them by surprise, I hope. Shoot them all. Don't let any of them get away."

Sullivan checked his pistol again just to be sure he had six bullets ready. He spit on the ground. He was a little nervous like any man is who is about to enter a battle. He was not scared, just a little anxious to get on with it.

As Boyd got closer to the camp, he stopped for a few moments to listen. He moved forward, stopped, listened, moved forward, stopped, listened, moved forward, stopped, listened.

He could see the smoke rising from the camp. He could smell it now. He was almost there. Maybe they have caught them eating, he thought. That would be good. They would not be near their weapons most likely.

He saw no guards on duty. That was strange, but like the Rangers, they probably pulled in their guards when the sun came up.

He listened intently again. He heard nothing. There was no talking, no noise, no ponies making any noise. That was really strange. They ought to be milling around their camp, making some kind of noise.

He went a little further, and then he saw it . . . .. the Comanche camp.

It was empty. They were all gone.

Boyd walked back toward the Rangers. When he got to where they could see him, he waved his arm, signaling them to come on to him.

In a few moments, he said, "They're gone, Sullivan."

"We're too late?"

"Yep."

"I was afraid of that. We'll have to keep after them. All right, Boys," Sullivan said, as he turned back toward the men, "we'll have to go chase'em down. Take us away, Boyd."

Boyd galloped off to the west in pursuit of the Comanches, following their tracks. The Rangers followed him and them.

Two hours later, Boyd came back to them.

"You ain't gonna like what I found. They hit a ranch house down just beyond that rise way down there," Boyd said, as he pointed off to the west.

"Take us there," Sullivan responded.

Boyd turned his horse around as Sullivan and the company fell in behind him.

Soon they came to a rise. They stopped to look. Far down below the rise, in a large level area, they could see the smoke rising from a house that had quickly burned to the ground. They were too far away to see anything else.

Sullivan did not need to see. He knew what was there. He had seen it many times before, too many times. He knew what it would look like, what had happened, what they would find.

"Let's go take a look," Sullivan said.

The Rangers rode down the long hill. As they got closer, they could see several bodies lying on the ground. There were no horses or cattle anywhere to be seen.

When they reached what was left of the house, they got off of their horses. They began looking at the bodies. There was one man, one woman, two small boys, and one small girl.

They had all been killed with bullets. Then they were stripped of their clothing, scalped, slit open from their abdomens up almost to their throats.

The Rangers stood there looking at them. They were speechless, almost not believing what they saw, yet knowing it was real. They were looking at it, wondering how any humans could do this to any other humans.

"All right, get the shovels. Get'em in the ground. Over there beyond the barn, I guess. Don't matter to them, I know. That's as good a place as any," Sullivan said.

As the Rangers began digging the graves, Boyd called out to Sullivan.

"Come look at this, would ya."

"What is it?"

"Something very interesting, Sullivan."

They stood looking at the ground and at all the tracks, those of the ponies, those of the Comanches, and then Boyd pointed to something else.

"Look at that," he said. "Amongst all the moccasin tracks are those right there. Somebody was barefoot. And look at them. Looks to me like it might be a female, maybe a girl in her teens or maybe a young woman."

"Yeah. Caught totally off-guard with no time to even put on her shoes. This complicates what we need to do, but at the same time it makes it even more urgent, more important."

"Think we can catch them in time?"

"Time for what?" asked Sullivan.

"You know."

"Yeah. All we can do is try. Maybe at least we can save her life, if not her dignity. We'll see, but we better get moving soon as we can."

"I'll get the Boys to hurry along."

"Good," Sullivan replied, as he kept looking at the young lady's footprints.

After a few minutes, Sullivan walked over to where the graves were being dug. This was nothing new to him, or the other men either. They had all seen this kind of thing before. But it was something no man in his right mind could ever get used to. It was savage, horrible, almost unbelievable, yet when a man saw it and watched the graves being dug and the bodies put in them, he knew it was real. It could not be denied. Worse yet, it could never be forgotten. And then there was another problem, for it would begin to work on a man on the inside, eat away at him, and never go away.

When the task was completed, Sullivan called the men together.

Boyd read the twenty-third psalm.

"Somebody pray," Sullivan said.

There was silence. None of them were used to praying in public, certainly not at a time like that.

Then Tommy Jackson cleared his throat and spoke.

"God, they are yours. We give them back to you. Welcome them home. And make things better for them than they were down here. Amen."

"Thanks, Tommy," Sullivan said. "Well, Boys, we found over yonder the footprints of a girl or maybe a young woman. They took her. So we got to not only kill'em all, we got to save her in the midst of all that. Might be tricky, but we'll do what we can. Mount up."

Chapter 12

Ranger Boyd again headed out following the unshod pony tracks. They were headed due west, toward God only knew what and where.

Sullivan and the Company followed him. They rode as fast as they could without exhausting their horses. They were in a barren land where there were no horses to replace theirs, so they had to beware of moving too fast.

About noon, they saw Boyd coming back toward them. Sullivan signaled the Company to stop and wait on him. Soon he came up to where they were waiting.

His first words were, "I don't know Sullivan."

"What is it?" Sullivan asked.

"I can tell by their tracks they're moving really fast. I don't know how we'll ever catch up to'em."

"Really fast, eh?"

"Really fast. Ya think they knew where we was back there where we camped? And they know we are coming after them?" Boyd asked.

"Oh, they knew, Boyd. And they knew we would be following them. That's why they left out so early. They wanted to get out ahead of us. And that ranch they hit. They could have gone on by it and left those people alone. But they went there anyway to kill those people and burn that house just to show us who they are and that they are superior to us. They were taunting us."

"So you think they're leading us on to somewhere?"

"Sure they are. And you won't need to be afraid they will kill you as soon as they see ya. Nope. They'll be out there somewhere waiting and when they see you, they'll know we will soon be comin' along."

"That means we do what?"

"We ain't got much of a choice. I guess we can do what I have done before."

"What's that?"

"Back in the war, our Army in Georgia was waiting on Sherman to come down out of Chattanooga. I lived up near there, by the way. But old Sherman was too smart. He kept going around them to the west. Kept trying to avoid them whenever he could. There was lots of battles, of course. But so many times when our Rebs dug in, he would turn toward the west, going around them. When they saw that, they would pull out and move further on down. It was like that all the way to Atlanta. You can bet they are watching us, at least now and then. I bet they are sending out scouts like we are sending you, just to keep an eye on where we are and what we're doing. They might be watching us right now. Who knows?"

"This means what for us?" Boyd asked.

"Well, I'm thinking. I'm thinking. Bickers, come up here closer."

When Bickers pulled up beside Sullivan and Boyd, Sullivan then spoke to them both.

"Here's what I'm thinking. Maybe we split up. Send part of us straight after them so they will know where we are. But the other half of us goes on around to the north a ways and then heads west. We try to get ahead of them. That means we, and I am saying I take that group, it means we don't stop for the night. We just keep on going. Boyd, you keep on the point so they will see you. Bickers, we think they know where we are and they're leading us on. Then, Bickers, you take your group straight after Boyd. How does that sound to y'all?"

They both thought a minute. Then Bickers spoke.

"Anything we do is risky. I'd soon die one way as another. And who knows, this just might work like magic."

"I agree," Boyd added.

"Now, we got to remember, they got the girl. We got to get her away from them one way or another."

"How we gonna do that?" Bickers asked.

"All of this is off the top of my head," Sullivan said. "Well, y'all don't camp tonight either. When the sun goes down, Boyd, you wait on them to catch up to you. Then just keep on going. You won't ride right into them because you'll see their fires from afar off.

I hope we will both be in place by dawn. When the sun comes up, y'all ride in shootin'. The sun will be in their eyes, so let it get up enough for that. Then once they are occupied with you, me and my Boys will come at them from their right side or from behind them."

Both men agreed to the plan. Then Sullivan chose the men who would go with him.

"Warner, Hunt, Wainwright, Summers, Long, come with me."

Then turning back to Boyd and Bickers, "Remember crack of dawn, but let the sun get up enough to blind them . . . . You Boys, follow me."

Sullivan and the men with him rode off to the north. They went about a mile, then turned back to the west.

Boyd went ahead due west, following the Indian pony tracks. Bickers and the others waited a few moments, letting Boyd get out ahead of them. Then they followed him.

Both groups rode hard that afternoon toward the place where the sun went down behind the hills and the mountains beyond.

In less than two hours, the light began to fade, the shadows began to lengthen, and the sky to the west began changing colors. There were streaks of yellow, pink, and red.

Bickers and his group caught up with Boyd, who was waiting on them. When they reached him, Boyd spoke first.

"Well, Boys, we are now gonna be sailing in the dark. Let's just hope they'll have a good fire goin' so we won't stumble into them."

"I'm countin' on it," Bickers replied. "Bettin' my life on it."

"Ain't we all."

A little further north, Sullivan and his group move west with determination. Darkness or no darkness, it did not matter to Sullivan. Just so they caught up with them. That was all that mattered.

Sullivan kept thinking about the girl or young woman, whatever she was. He knew what they would do with her. Probably each Indian would rape her. Then they might just kill her on the spot. More of the game they were playing to show the Rangers they could and would do anything they wanted. They also might decide to let her live so they could take her to their village and either make a slave out of her or someone's wife. Slave or wife, it would be a hard life. Maybe, just maybe, they could reach them in time to save her. Maybe they could find a way to get her out so she is not killed in all the gunfire and they do not kill her when they realize what is happening.

They were taking a chance, he knew that. But they had no choice, he also knew that. They would just do the best they could. They had to risk it.

Chapter 13

The night was long and dark. The moon was hiding somewhere behind some clouds, and few stars dared to show their faces. It was as if all of nature was aware of something terrible about to take place.

It would have been better for both groups of Rangers if there had been a night when the moon was bigger and brighter. But they had no control over that, and therefore it was not something for them to fret about. They just rode west, that was all they could do and all they needed to do. The details would take care of themselves. Anyway, with it so dark, they were safer, more difficult to be seen, less likely to be a target for some Comanche out there on guard waiting on them.

After three hours, Sullivan told his men to halt. They had come to a little creek.

"Let yore horses drink. We need to stretch our legs anyway. We can't ride all night and not stop to rest."

They all dismounted and led their horses to the water. Some tied their horses to the limbs of small trees and then peed in the bushes.

In the distance, they could not tell how far, they heard the sound of coyotes howling in the night.

After fifteen minutes, Sullivan said, "All right, let's get back at it."

They mounted up, crossed the creek, and continued toward the unfolding west.

They stopped to rest two more times. On that second time, Sullivan spoke to the men about what they should do.

"From now on, I want you, Johnny Hunt, to go about a half a mile down to the south. Don't go too far. But then turn west again. Keep yore eyes out for camp fires. You'll be close enough to see'em I'm guessing. When you spot them, come back and get us. We'll get close enough so that when the sun comes up, we can join the others in the attack. Got it?"

"Got it."

"Now, while we're killin' Indians, I want you Ben Long, to find that girl. Don't worry about them except to defend yoreself. Yore job is to get her and get out of there as quick as you can. Head out to the east. If the rest of us don't make it, you keep going with her. Get her to safety somewhere. But don't take her back to the ranch. She don't need to see all that. Just tell her we took care of her family in a proper way."

"Sure."

"Let's move out."

Almost two hours later, Johnny Hunt came riding toward them as fast as his horse would go.

"Sarge, they're down there in a little valley like place, right on a creek. They got three big fires blazin'. We can't miss'em."

"All right, Boys. Sun'll be up pretty soon. This is it. Now keep quiet when we get close. No noise of any kind, not from horses, bridles, saddles, nothin'. Let's go."

The Rangers dismounted and led their horses toward the Indian camp. Soon they were where they could see the fires.

Sullivan held up his hand, as he whispered, "We'll wait for the others to attack."

They stood there waiting as the deep darkness began to move out toward the west and lighter sky began slipping in from the east. Soon all the sky around and over them was gray. Looking toward the east they could see streaks of light across the horizon.

Sullivan nodded his head upward as he got back up on his horse. The other Rangers mounted up. He pulled his pistol out from under his ammo belt that was around his waist. The other Rangers drew their pistols.

They looked toward the east. The sky was brighter now. Minutes later, the sun was peeping up over the distant hills. Brighter and brighter and brighter it became. Then it was glaring, almost blinding the Rangers as they looked at it.

Bang!

Pow!

Bang!

Bang!

Pow!

Pow!

"Let's go!" Sullivan shouted.

They galloped in from the north as Bickers and his men attacked from the east!

The Comanches were caught off guard!

Comanches rushed out of their sleep from under their blankets, having been lying on the ground!

They fell dead!

Some Comanches grabbed their rifles and began to fire back!

One by one Comanches hit the ground!

The Rangers kept shooting them!

Some Comanches began running for their ponies!

Rangers followed them out the west end of their camp and shot them down dead!

Indian ponies ran away with no riders on them!

The shooting stopped. It was all over. Thirty-four Comanches lay dead on the ground.

The women and children and old men had vanished. They had run off into the brush and taken cover, thinking the white men would kill them as well.

Ben Long came riding back into the camp from the east. The girl was on the back of his horse with her arms around him.

By then, the Rangers were making sure the battle was really over.

When Long and the girl dismounted, the Rangers saw this was no girl. She was a full-grown woman.

Long had helped her off the horse, and then they walked toward where Sullivan was.

All the Rangers had dismounted and were looking around the camp. Some of them wanted to see what kind of weapons and trinkets they could find. Some were looking at furs and winter clothing made from them.

Best of all they found fresh meat which they needed.

They left those furs and all the things they knew the women, children, and old people would need. They also left most of the fresh meat, only taking a small amount of it.

They found a couple of small children wandering around, having been left in the panic of the moment. They picked them up and tried to comfort them as they looked beyond the camp for their mothers.

Chapter 14

The Rangers looked at the young woman. Her dress was torn and dirty. She had no shoes. But they could see what a beautiful young lady she was with long blond hair and eyes of blue.

Sullivan walked over to her.

"We're Texas Rangers. I'm Toombs Sullivan, the leader of this group for right now. We was chasing the Comanches that hit yore place. They had attacked another company of ours and killed half of them. So we was out to get'em. What's yore name?"

"Augusta Browning."

"Sorry about what happened to yore family. We took care of them in a proper way.

Don't think ya ought to go back there. Ain't nothin' left but the barn. Didn't see no stock of any kind. Ya couldn't make it there by yoreself."

"I know . . . . I know. Thanks for saving my life. I've heard what they do to women captives."

"Did they . . . .? Sorry. None of my business."

"Yes, they did. I don't mind telling you. I'm just glad you got to me before they killed me or took me to their people and made me a slave or a bride. If I have a baby, I'll have no idea who the father is. They passed me around."

"Sorry."

"Don't be sorry. You saved me."

"Well, we got to get you somewhere that you'll be safe. You got any kin anywhere?"

"No, not out here in Texas. Got some back east. South Carolina."

"We're gonna be heading east back toward the coast. All we can do is bring you along with us, and try to find you a town where somebody can help ya."

"That's fine."

"All right," he answered her. Then he said, "Some of you boys see if ya can round up one of them Indian ponies. This young lady needs a ride."

Soon they were on their way back toward where they had intended to go.

They rode hard all that day, stopping several times for the good of the horses and for their own good as well.

The Rangers noticed that Augusta Browing was very experienced at riding horses. She took to the Indian pony like it was her own and she had always ridden it.

Late that evening, they came to the San Antonio River where they made a camp. As usual, the first thing they did was let the horses and the Rangers drink from the river. Then they tied off the horses, built fires, and began getting a meal together. They started cooking some of the fresh meat they had gotten from the Indian camp. They were not sure what it was, but they would know when they tasted it.

Sullivan noticed that Augusta Browning seemed to be lost. She had that far away look, that empty stare at nothing. She was standing in the middle of the camp area. He walked over to her.

"I'm guessing you might like to get cleaned up. This river is the only place, but it's a good place. We'll stand guard and nobody will look. And I think we can put together some clothes for you to wear. Men's clothes, of course. We don't carry around nothin' for women."

"Oh, yes. Thanks. Men's clothes are just fine. You should see the way I dress at the ranch for chores . . . . used to dress, I mean. I looked like a man when I put on a hat."

"I'm sorry about your family. We all are. Hadn't had a chance to tell you that till now."

"Thanks. I haven't had a chance for what happened to them to sink in yet. I was so expecting to die and was so caught up in all that, that I have not even had time to cry or mourn. It will all become real, and I will be a total mess."

"I know. You've a right to do that. Any time you need to talk or need to stop on our journey, just let us know. We'd be glad to help you any way we can."

"Thanks for that."

Turning away from her, he said, "Boyd! Come escort this young lady to the public bath, but don't let it be public. And get somebody to find her some clothes to wear."

The Rangers found amongst them a small shirt and some pants that looked like they would fit. From the things the mules had carried, they found an extra set of boots and a hat. Boyd gathered it all up in his arms.

"Follow me," he said to Augusta Browning

Boyd led her down the river about a hundred yards. When they stopped, he spoke to her.

"This'll be as good a place as any. Can't nobody see ya here. I'll turn around and look the other way. Here's yore new clothes right here. Well, they ain't new, but they'll do, I hope."

"They'll be just fine. Thanks for your kindness."

"Yes. Ma-am," Boyd said, as he walked away back toward the camp a few yards.

Augusta Browning stepped over near the river. She unbuttoned her dress and let it fall to the ground. She was not wearing anything else. She picked it up and tossed it over in the bushes.

She slowly walked to the edge of the water, put her right foot in it, and then went on in up to her waist. She immersed herself, letting the water cover her head, and swam out ten yards. The water was cold, but it was cleansing and refreshing. She came back in to where she could sit down. She sloshed the water up all over her body. It was good. She was beginning to feel like a human being again.

Ten minutes later, she came back up out of the water. She then knew she needed something to dry herself with. There was only one thing to do, use the old torn dress.

When she was dressed, she walked toward Boyd saying, "I'm ready now. Thanks again."

"Sure thing."

The two of them walked back to the camp. The meal was ready. They took plates and helped themselves to the beans, bread, and beef. It was meat from Augusta's family 's ranch. Then they poured coffee in cups. They went over to where Sullivan was seated on the ground. They sat down beside him.

"Feel better?" Sullivan asked.

"Yes, on the outside," she replied. "But some things you cannot wash away, things on the inside."

"Yeah, I know all about that. I tried it. It don't work. Don't work."

"No."

Then Sullivan said, "Bickers, you and Boyd post the guards for the night. Two-hour shifts, like always."

"Sure, Boss," Boyd answered.

"You bet," Bickers added.

Sullivan turned to Augusta and looked at her for a moment. He thought he might get her mind off of what had just happened to her.

"Tell me about living in Carolina."

"Not much to tell really. We lived not too far from Augusta, Georgia. That's how I got my name. We had a really nice farm, grew cotton, and then took it to Augusta. Yes, we had slaves. About twenty I'd say. Varied at times. When the slaves were set free, most of them left. A few stayed out of a sense of loyalty or something. It was already hard times, what with the war and all. This about finished us off. Then the Yankees came and burned down our house. Daddy had the foresight enough to hide our big wagon and the mules in the woods. Not long after that the war was over. We loaded up anything that was left and came out here. That's about it."

"I thought you said not much to tell. That was quite a bit of much."

"You grow up here in Texas?"

"Oh, no. I had a farm in north-west Georgia, up near Chattanooga. Not much to tell. Lost it with the war too. Came out here. That's it."

Augusta Browning sensed there was quite a bit more to tell, but she did not want to press Sullivan for it. She thought there must be things he just does not want to say.

Soon the men began turning in. It had been a long and difficult day of riding. They needed rest and sleep. They hoped the rest would come soon, and maybe the sleep as well.

Early the next morning, they were up and at it again, getting a quick breakfast together, gulping down scalding hot coffee, saddling the horses, loading the mules, and then heading off to the east again.

After they had been gone three minutes, a hand reached down into the bushes by the river and pulled out a dirty torn dress. The Comanche Indian looked at it, then held it up for the others still on their ponies to see.

Chapter 15

Once again, Boyd was riding point, going a few miles out ahead of the others.

After a couple of hours, Bickers, who had been beside Sullivan all along, looked over at him and spoke.

"I keep gettin' the feelin' we're being followed."

"That's because we are. More Comanches, I would be willin' to bet. Must have been some of'em out on a hunting party in the other direction overnight, maybe lookin' for game or somethin'."

"After they found what we did to their band, I'm guessing they're gonna be really mad about it.'

"Hopin' mad. Blood-thirsty mad, I'd say."

"They'll not only want revenge, they'll want the woman back too."

"Yep. Ya see that little hill up there. When we go over it, you stay back and see if ya can get a look at'em. I'd like to know how many of'em are back there."

"All right."

As soon as the Rangers went over the hill, Bickers held up his horse, jumped off, and tied him to a tree. He then slipped back up the hill bending low to the ground. He hid behind a bush and looked through the limbs and leaves. In a few moments, he saw them.

He wasted no time in catching up with the company and telling Sullivan what he saw.

"They're back there, a few minutes behind us. Don't seem to be in no big hurry, but just keepin' pace with us, maybe waiting till we stop to camp."

"How many?"

"It was hard to tell. I didn't want to sit there and count. But I'd say as many of them as of us. Maybe twenty, twenty-five."

"We gonna do to them what they did to us. Let's speed up and give ourselves a little time to get situated. Let's go, Boys! Hang on, Lady!"

The Rangers rode hard and fast for several miles, gaining a little time.

Soon they came to a deep ravine along a creek-bed. They went straight through it to the far end. Then they hid their horses.

"Take cover on both sides!" Sullivan said. "Some of you climb up top, both sides!"

Sullivan took Augusta Browning's hand and led her to the right side.

"You stay down behind me."

"I can shoot."

"I don't doubt it. The extra Winchesters we got are tied down to the mules. They are the ones that belonged to the Rangers these Indians killed. We ain't got time to get them. I got mine here. My other rifle is a Sharps. Takes a little time to reload, so I need this one for myself. If I fall, you take it up, quick. Here, take this pistol."

Sullivan pulled his pistol from under his belt and handed it to her.

"I had noticed you don't wear a belt with a holster like most of the others."

"Nope. Too bulky for me. Ain't got time to fool with that."

"How long until they get here?"

"Should be along just any old time now."

Sullivan looked back up the ravine, but he saw nothing.

The sweat ran down his face. He lifted up his right arm and wiped it on his sleeve.

"Won't be long now, Boys," he said in a low voice.

They waited as the seconds felt like minutes and the minutes felt like hours and the hours that were minutes seemed to stop dead still.

Suddenly they saw one Comanche on his pony stopped still at the mouth of the ravine.

He sat there looking and listening. He turned sideways and signaled the others to come along. They pulled beside him and stopped.

As they advanced into the ravine, shots rang out behind the Rangers!

Half of the Comanches had circled around!

They were behind them!

And the ones in front were charging now!

On they came firing their rifles at the Rangers!

And the ones behind were charging also!

The Rangers were caught in a vice-grip of flying lead hitting all around them and striking some of them!

The Rangers were firing back!

Bang!

Bang!

Bang!

Pow!

Pow!

Pow!

Bang!

Pow!

Bang!

Indians were falling off their horses all around!

Falling in the creek!

Falling in the mud!

No time for the Rangers to reload their empty rifles!

They threw them to the ground!

They pulled out their pistols!

Pow!

Pow!

Pow!

Pow!

Sullivan took the pistol from Augusta!

Pow!

Pow!

Pow!

Then it was over. Many Indians were dead on the ground. Some of their ponies were wandering around looking like they were lost. Other ponies ran away in both directions. Some of the Comanches had retreated and gone back where they came from. But most of them would never go back to their families.

The Rangers did not bother to count how many were dead. Instead, they looked to their own.

Three Rangers were dead. Ollie Reynolds and Young John West of Company J, and Buck Johnson of Sullivan's Company L had been killed.

William Boyd came riding up. He had heard the distant shots.

"Well now," was all he said.

"You missed the party," Sullivan said.

"Looks like ya had a good time. And I don't think you needed me from what I see lying around here on the ground"

"We lost three men. Reynolds, West, Johnson."

"I'm sorry."

"Yeah."

Sullivan looked away for a moment.

"All right, Boys. You know what to do. Let's get'em in the ground. And take'em out of this ravine, out in the open where they can breathe and enjoy the wind and the sun."

The Rangers took their shovels from the mules, dug the graves, placed their friends in the them.

Bickers read the twenty-third psalm.

Boyd said a prayer.

"Heavenly Father, receive these Boys. They were good ones. We entrust them to you, Amen."

The Rangers left as soon as they could.

They left the Comanches lying on the ground. Dead. In the sun.

Chapter 16

The Rangers headed for Corpus Christi. It was the closest town of any size. Sullivan thought Augusta Browning's chances were better there than anywhere else in that part of Texas.

The name of that town means the Body of Christ. The bay was first discovered by Spanish explorer Alonso Alvarez in 1519 on the feast day of Corpus Christi. The first permanent settlement had been built in 1839.

After three days of hard riding, the Rangers arrived at the town. They went straight to a hotel and checked in. Then they took their horses and mules down the street to a livery stable.

A good night in a hotel would be a welcomed relief from the hard living of camping every night and eating what they had or could kill. They were almost a hundred and fifty miles and several days from San Antonio, their last night in civilization. It would be especially good for Augusta Browning.

After they had all cleaned up, they went to the hotel's dining room. Augusta Browning sat at a table with Sullivan, Boyd, and Bickers.

"This is a nice town. I've never been here before," Augusta said.

"Yeah," Sullivan replied. "Uh, it ain't no accident that we came here. You got options here."

"Options?" she asked.

"Options. You can stay here. You could catch a stage coach up to San Antonio, Dallas, Austin. You could also catch a ship to Charleston, you havin' kin in South Carolina."

"I have no idea if any of our folk in Carolina survived the war. We've not heard from any of them in years. Besides, even if I knew anything about any of them, I have nothing there to go to, no future in Carolina. Texas is my home, even though I don't have a home in Texas now, still this is where I belong."

"I understand. I could never go back to Georgia. Too much to forget and not much I want to remember. So what will you do?"

"I have no idea."

Sullivan reached in his pocket, pulled out fifty dollars, and said, "You take this. It ain't much. But it'll help ya do somethin'. You could stay here a while, travel north, or take a boat if ya change yore mind about Carolina."

"Thanks so much. But I hate to take your money."

"Ya quite welcome, but it ain't my money. It's Ranger money given for any needed expenses. In the mornin', we'll go over to the store and buy you some female clothes and something to put them in when ya travel. I still got more expense money," he said with a smile.

"I can't thank you enough."

"You thanked me enough."

After the meal, Augusta Browning went up to her room. The days of hard travel had caught up with her.

Sullivan did the same thing, along with several other Rangers. The rest of them went down the street to one of the saloons.

The next morning, all the horses and the mules were lined up outside of the hotel. The men were checking their saddles and gear, and making sure the packs on the mules were secure.

Augusta Browning had been taken by Sullivan to a store where he bought her two dresses, shoes, a travel bag, combs and brushes, and several other things she needed.

As they left the store, she turned to Sullivan.

"I want to thank you for your kindness. You didn't have to do this, buying me all these items."

"You needed them, right?"

"Yes, I had nothing but Ranger clothes. I didn't look like a very good Ranger, did I?"

"Well, you were close, but not very close," he said, with a laugh.

"So you're riding off to chase bad men?"

"Yes, we are."

"When you catch them, what then?"

"Generally, we give them a chance to be good men or we kill 'em."

"Does it ever wear on you, all the killing?"

"Try not to think about it. It's like with those Comanches. There was no choice about it. It is not a moral question, right or wrong, should we, should we not. Our job is to stop them. They kill. We kill. If we don't kill them, then they kill more. It's a mean country we live in out here in Texas. It ain't refined like New York, Boston, or even Atlanta or Charleston. You want to stay alive? You do what ya have to do. Plain and simple."

"I guess so. I might not have understood that before all that happened to us. But I see it now."

They reached the hotel.

"Well, you go on upstairs and get into those new clothes."

She hurried up to her room to change clothes to see them off.

When she came back downstairs and out to the board sidewalk, the Rangers saw her and clapped their hands. She smiled and twirled around.

"Well, this is goodbye," Sullivan said.

"Yes, I know." Then she said to all of them, "Thank y'all so much. You saved my life. I am aware of that very much so. If you had not come along, I hate to think what would have happened to me."

The Rangers smiled and nodded, not knowing what to say to her, but they knew very well what she said was true.

"Well, this is goodbye," Sullivan said again awkwardly.

Augusta Browning smiled at him.

"Maybe I'll see ya again," he said.

"Maybe so."

"How will I find you?"

"If I decide to leave here, I'll leave word with the hotel owner about where I'm going. But, who knows, I might just stay here."

"Good."

Then Sullivan turned to the men, and said, "Let's get on down the road, Boys."

He mounted his horse, tipped his hat at Augusta Browning, and led them down the street headed south. As they began that journey, Sullivan was thinking, what was I saying that for? I tried that twice already and it never works out. All it brings is disaster. I need to just think about the work at hand. Period.

Chapter 17

It was another one hundred and fifty miles down to Brownsville. That was the last town on the border with Mexico, one hundred and fifty hot and dusty miles.

Sullivan knew they would reach the eight hundred-thousand-acre ranch owned by Captain Horace Charles Roland long before they got to Brownsville, but he did not know where the man lived on that vast spread of land.

After three days of hard riding, the Rangers came to an area of obvious grazing land with hundreds of cows scattered everywhere they looked. There was no doubt they had reached the Roland Ranch.

Soon they saw some ranch hands. Boyd rode over to them, telling them who the Rangers were, and asking where could they find Captain Roland. He came right back with the directions.

"This is the right place. All them cattle got a big R R burned on'em. We got about thirty miles to go. We'll see his house and other houses, barns and all that straight ahead. We'll be there long before sun-down."

"Good," Sullivan replied.

The Rangers spent the rest of that day heading toward the house where Roland lived.

At almost five o'clock in the afternoon, they came up over a rise and paused to look.

"Would you look at that," Bickers said.

"Yea," Sullivan answered. "Some kind of modest ranch house."

They sat there for a few minutes, looking at what lay before them. There was a large two-story house that looked like it belonged in Austin on one of its most fashionable streets. There were porches wrapping around both stories, four chimneys, ornate doors and windows. It was made of red brick. There were seven small houses for ranch hands, a row of out-houses, four large barns, coral areas, and three wind-mills for pumping water from the wells. Large stockyards were near the barns.

"I ain't never seen nothing like this," said Tommy Jackson.

"I don't guess any of us ever have either," answered Sullivan. "I've seen similar houses back home in Georgia, but nothing like this, nothing this vast."

"What kind of man are we about to meet?" asked Boyd.

"A very successful one," replied Sullivan. "Well, let's get on with it."

They rode down the rise toward the mansion. They went through a gate that had two large letters over it – R R. They stopped in front of the big house and dismounted. No sooner had they gotten off their horses when a man came out the front door. Not knowing what or who to expect, they were not sure who this person was, a ranch hand, a house man, a foreman maybe.

They looked up at him as he stood on the porch, a few steps above them. He was tall, thin, rugged, browned by the sun. He had a brown mustache, brown hair with some white mixed in that was just over his shirt collar. He wore a faded red shirt, worn looking jeans tucked into his old dirty boots.

Sullivan started to ask if Captain Roland was around, but thought better of it.

"I'm Roland," the man said, in a rough sounding voice.

"I'm Toombs Sullivan, Texas Rangers."

"Figgered as much. Been expectin' ya. Hope ya had a not too eventful trip down here from Austin."

"It was quite eventful. I'll tell ya 'bout it when we have a chance to talk."

"Good. I expect ya might like to settle in and clean up. Yore house is the last on the line down there. Supper is at seven. Come back up here then."

"Right," Sullivan answered.

Captain Roland turned around and went back inside.

"Ain't like no rich man I ever saw," said Bickers.

"No, he ain't," Sullivan replied. "He obviously earned it all and did not inherit any of it."

The Rangers walked their horses to a coral, put their saddles in the barn, and then took their saddlebags, rifles, and any other gear with them into the last little house at the end of the line. There were enough double-bed bunks for all of them. Each man claimed the one he wanted.

"Reckon what we got ourselves into?" Boyd asked Sullivan.

Sullivan smiled at him as he pitched his hat up on a top bunk.

"You might recall, we didn't get ourselves into this. We were sent here to do a job."

"What do you make of that man? With all he has here, you'd think he could protect himself."

"Yeah, I know. We'll find out what kind of man he is real soon."

When the Rangers came back to the house for the meal, they were shown into a large dining room by a Mexican woman. Before them was a long table set for them.

"Take ya seats, Gentlemen," Roland thundered, as he came into the room from back in the kitchen.

The Rangers sat down, and immediately large platters were placed in front of each of them containing a steak, rice, beans, tomatoes, bread, and then wine was served to them.

They began eating like they had not had food in a long time. There was little conversation except between Roland and Sullivan.

"Guess you were well informed about why I wanted you to come down here?"

"I think so. Cattle rustlers from Mexico."

"Yeah. And the worst kind. They don't take them to be sold to feed anybody. They just slaughter them to get the tallow from the skins. They send it off to Cuba where they make candles out of it. A big market."

"So I was told."

"That Mexican General, former General, has his own private army. General Fernado Antonio De Vega. Has a bunch of other names, middle names, middle middle names. I can't remember. My boys are tough. They can fight. They're Texans, but they are not soldiers. Besides we can't leave our cattle alone to go off and find other cattle that have been stolen. Then none would be protected. See what I mean?"

"I do."

"That's why you are here. I'll take you and your men out tomorrow and show what we are up against, what they do. You'll get a taste of it. Bad choice of words. A smell of it."

"Good. How long has this been goin' on?"

"Oh, about two years. I'm thinking he has been doing this kind of thing for a while. His operation is so smooth. But he discovered us. We have so many head he just could not resist. He is like a kid at the store, standing in front of all that candy. The fact that he cannot have any of it makes it all that more alluring. So he steals a piece of it and runs home to Mama."

"How many men does he have?"

"I don't know for sure, but the rumor is there are about fifty. That means there could be thirty and there could be a hundred."

"Let's hope it's not a hundred."

"Yes. Tell me about yourself."

Sullivan gave him a brief history of his life without telling anything really personal because Roland did not need to know all that and he did not want to go through it.

After the meal, they all retired to Roland's front porch where they drank more wine and watched the sun go down.

Chapter 18

After a hearty breakfast of steak, eggs, bacon, biscuits, gravy, beans, and coffee the next morning, Roland led the Rangers out on a trip to see the dead cattle.

None of the Rangers had ever seen such a ranch before. It was miles and miles of grazing land and woods and scrub and creeks and hills and low places. Nor had they ever seen so many cattle. There were thousands scattered all over the part of the ranch they saw. And the deer were everywhere, big bucks and many does. Each time the Rangers came over a rise or a hill the deer scattered, but the cows and bulls just looked at them, but not for long for they were not impressed.

They rode about ten miles before coming to the site of the slaughter. They had seen the circling of the buzzards far back before they arrived. When they came to within three hundred yards of the site, Roland held up his left hand.

"Stop right here. We don't need to get any closer. There must be about two hundred head of cattle lying there in the sun. You can see the piles of skins lying all around. And look at all that rotten meat. Just lying there. What a waste."

The Rangers formed a line as they pulled up closer so they could see.

Now they watched the buzzards as they hopped around among the dead corpses eating whatever they wanted. The aroma was breath-taking. They could almost see the odor rising in the air.

"They scrape the tallow off those skins, then just toss them aside. Comanches don't do this kind of thing. I know that some of them will sneak into my land and take a few cows now and then so they can feed their families. I don't mind that. I don't mind as much as this the ones that will steal maybe a hundred or so to sell or trade. At least they don't go to waste. But this is waste. It is senseless."

"I see what ya mean," responded Sullivan.

"General De Vega is making tons and tons of money off this. Nobody in Cuba cares what he is doing as long as they can do business together."

"What men will do for money," Sullivan said.

"They will do anything for money. Just anything," Roland replied.

"And they will kill anybody and anything to get it."

"I want this stopped. But you won't stop it by killing a few of De Vega's men. I've done that, tried that. No matter how many are killed, he has more. More and more. Ya have to cut off the head of the snake. That's the only way. I want that man dead. Period."

Sullivan turned and looked at Roland. He thought a moment and then spoke.

"We'll kill'im all right. But it's gonna take some doin'. There's twenty of us, and he's got an army. Getting to him might be a problem, a big problem."

"You've seen here what he does. You're beginning to understand that problem. He is well insulated."

"Yes, he is. But there's a way to get to him. There's always a way."

"That's what I like to hear," replied Roland, with a smile. "Let's get out of here."

They arrived back at the mansion about mid-afternoon.

As they all dismounted, Roland said, "I've got some book-keeping to catch up on before I get too far behind. Make yourselves at home. Supper same time and place."

A ranch hand came and got Roland's horse and led him to a barn. Roland climbed up the front steps and disappeared inside.

"All right, Boys," Sullivan said, "let's put up our horses. Then we need to get a little rest, and also get our guns and gear ready. We got a big day tomorrow. We're goin' huntin'."

When they went to their quarters, some of the Rangers got on their beds and went to sleep. Others gathered around small tables and played cards.

Late in the evening, they all washed up, combed their hair, and got ready for the evening meal. It was basically the same kind of food they had the night before.

After the meal, the Rangers sat around the table and listened to Roland as he talked about the war with Mexico and what he did in it while on the river. He told of his friendship with General Zachery Taylor and how he supplied him with all he needed.

"Those were wonderful days, days of adventure, especially for a young man out looking for adventure. And I found it too, found it all. But the real adventure began for me when I saw this land, bought it, and started raising cattle. There is nothing like it. I have everything I could ever want. I say to one go and he goes, and to another come and he comes. I have loyal people who work for me with the cattle out on the range and here around the yards and here in this house."

After listening a while, Sullivan had a question.

"What about our war with the North? What did you do and how did that affect you?"

"Well, I had long since sold my boat. Those days on the river were over years ago. But I did have something the South needed. Meat. I supplied, at a good price I might add, plenty of cattle for the cause. Some of them were herded north and some were shipped out of Brownsville to various places.

"Speaking of Brownsville, some of De Vega's men come up into town. They raise hell, drink, visit their women there. Then they'll go back across the border. I don't think De Vega himself ever comes up there. He is not stupid enough to do that, but he does buy a lot of his supplies there, his men that is. If you go there and keep your eyes open, you just might learn something. He does come into Texas on his raids. Lots of people, including some of my men, have seen him. I have not seen him. If I ever had, I would have killed him."

"How will we know him when we see him?"

"Oh, you will know him from what I have heard. He's all blast and thunder. Don't forget he was a general and he has never gotten over that. He still has a military presence about him. And his men treat him like he is still a general. Many of them, don't forget, were in the army with him, but not all of them. He has recruited regular civilians too. Well, let's go into the library for a little sherry."

Sullivan and his men followed Roland into a large room that had four walls of books, hundreds of them. There was also plenty of room for his gun collection. The Rangers looked at the rows of books and all the guns.

"Many of these weapons are from the war with Mexico. General Taylor gave me some of them. Others are from our recent fuss with the Yankees. Some of them I use for hunting. I have all the latest Winchesters and pistols and a pretty nice collection of knives over there."

The Rangers walked around the room looking at the books. None of them had ever seen such a collection. They inspected the many pistols and rifles and shotguns Roland had. They looked at the trophy bucks over the massive fireplace, five of them. There were trophy buffaloes and mountain goats all around the room.

Roland walked over to a cabinet which he opened and then poured a glass of sherry for each of the men. Then he stood before them, held up his glass and offered a toast.

"Here's to death."

Chapter 19

The next morning, the Rangers headed out to Brownsville. After they had ridden a few miles, Sullivan held up his hand and halted the column. The men circled around him.

"I been thinking about what we need to do when we get there," he said. "I think we best not announce ourselves. Let's go into town in twos and threes. We'll split up right here, and go at intervals of, say, five minutes or more. Me and Boyd will be last. Bickers, you and two men go in first. We'll meet tonight at the main saloon, the biggest, around nine o'clock. Get rooms at a hotel. If there's more than one, it'd be best if we ain't all in the same one. Listen a lot. See what you can find out. Bickers, you and a couple of ya go on now. Questions?"

Bickers, Jimmy Crabtree, and Billy Dunnagan headed out to Brownsville.

The others followed in pairs. Finally, Sullivan and Boyd headed that way.

When they arrived in the sleepy little town, they saw what appeared to them to be a mixture of cultures. They rode down the main street looking to the left and the right. They knew they were still in Texas, but it seemed like Mexico as well.

After putting their horses in a livery stable, Sullivan and Boyd went into a cafe.

It was the typical Texas cafe, but it was also different. It seemed like they were in Texas, but it seemed like it was also Mexico. It was a cafe, but it was also a saloon. They served steak like any Texas cafe, but also Mexican beans and peppers and onions. They served beer, but it was Mexican beer. They serve whiskey, but they also served tequila.

They had music, but there was no piano. It was all guitars like you might hear in Mexico.

They took seats at a table, and then ordered their meals. As they ate, they kept looking around, listening, wondering. They saw no one there who looked like a former member of the Mexican Army.

The waitress came over to pour more coffee for them. Sullivan looked up at her.

"Say, could I ask you a question?"

"You just did. Yes. What else?"

"Uh, it might be a little out of place."

"And?"

"I'm wondering about something."

"You seem to be. Is that all?"

"No. Do you ever have men from Mexico come in here?"

"Are you serious? I can throw a rock from right here into Mexico. Of course we do."

"We're wanting to know if ya have anybody who might have been in their army, you know, military lookin'."

"Now how would I know about military looking?"

"I'm not sure."

"Apparently not."

"Well, we're tryin' to find out about some men who come up here and steal cattle from the R R ranch."

"Why didn't you say so to start with. Yeah, I know about them. They come in here some."

"They do?"

"Yes, I said they do. But nobody says anything about that. They are afraid to say anything or act like they notice them."

"How often does this take place? Them comin' in here?"

"Real often. It's mostly on a Monday evening. I would assume that is before they are up to no-good. They wouldn't do their deeds and then come by here on the way back across. Know why I know that?"

"Why?"

"Because they don't bring a herd through town."

"Reckon not. That was easy."

"You both some kind of lawmen?"

"Oh, no. We're in the cattle business. Just wondering who we might buy from to ship out of here over to New Orleans."

"All right. If you say so. You look like lawmen to men. Anything else for you?"

"No, that'll be all. Enjoyed the meal. Here's ya money."

"Thanks. I'll tell the cook you liked it."

When the waitress walked away, Sullivan turned to Boyd.

"And just what is today, Boyd?"

"It's Monday."

"That means tomorrow is Tuesday. Unless I'm wrong, that is."

"You ain't wrong."

"Why don't we just sit here a while and see what comes through the door?"

An hour later, five men came into the cafe. They were obviously from Mexico, and looked out of place. They did not seem like other people of Mexican descent who lived in Brownsville. They walked up to a table on the other side of the room and sat down. The waitress walked over to them, speaking to them in Spanish. They ordered their meals in Spanish. As they waited on their food, they talked and laughed. Their clothing and boots were dusty looking. They appeared to have ridden a good way that day.

Sullivan and Boyd tried to appear they were not watching them, as they watched them.

They were sure these men were a part of the little cattle-stealing army they were looking for.

After the waitress served their food, she looked over at Sullivan and Boyd and winked at them.

"Let's go," Sullivan said.

At a little before nine o'clock, all the Rangers were gathered in the saloon. They sat at three tables in the back corner.

Sullivan asked, "Anything?"

Some of the men reported seeing several Mexicans who seemed to be what they were looking for in that saloon and in a couple of others.

Then Sullivan shared what he and Boyd had found. After describing them he said, "Be ready to go at first light. We'll follow these people out of town and see if we can catch them at their meanness."

Chapter 20

Early the next morning, while trying not to be too noticeable, the Rangers stood around on the street waiting for the suspected cattle rustlers to leave. They were scattered around, no more than two or three standing together. Their horses were still in the livery stable, but were saddled up. The mules were loaded.

"Wonder where they are?" Sullivan asked, as he leaned against a post in front of a general store.

"Maybe they had a long night," Boyd suggested.

"Must've been that Mexican tequila."

"They must have drunk all of it."

"Maybe so."

"Guess they 'll come along sooner or later," Boyd said.

"Looks like it's gonna be later."

They had been waiting since dawn, but it was nearly nine o'clock before they saw a group of ten or twelve Mexicans riding down the street, headed out the west side of town.

Sullivan said to Boyd, after they rode past them, "I think those are the ones we want to follow."

"Looks like it," Boyd replied.

"Hey, five of those are the ones we saw last night in that cafe."

"Well, that's them then."

"Let's get after them."

Sullivan waved at all the others. Then they headed for the stable.

As they were about to leave, Sullivan said, "We need to stay well back so they won't see us. Boyd, you take the point. Let us know when you see where they're going."

"Yep," Boyd said, as he rode out ahead of them.

Even though still early in the day, it was already hot. Hot and dusty. There had been little or no rain lately. The ground was parched. What grass there was looked like it was dying. The tracks of the cattle rustlers could be easily seen.

They knew they were on Roland's land. It was that vast. They were already seeing cattle.

Almost an hour later, they saw Boyd come riding back toward them.

"Just up ahead! They're moving cattle!"

"Let's go, Boys!" shouted Sullivan.

The Rangers rode fast with Boyd out front leading them!

They heard gun-shots!

Pow!

Pow!

Pow!

They came to a small valley a few minutes later. They had seen the dust rising before they got there.

A herd of cattle was stampeding headed straight south. At least thirty or forty Mexicans were all around them and behind them. They were firing their pistols in the air, pushing the cattle hard and fast.

The Rangers fell in after them, but they were too fast and too far ahead of them.

The Rangers began firing at the rustlers with their pistols and Winchesters!

Bang!

Pow!

Bang!

Bang!

Pow!

Pow!

Pow!

Two of the rustlers fell off their horses! The horses kept running fast and forward headed south!

Soon they came to the Rio Grande River.

The cattle and the rustlers never slowed down!

They ran right across and kept heading into Mexico!

When the Rangers reached the river, they stopped and watched the herd as it disappeared.

Sullivan got off his horse. Then the others did as well.

"Water your horses," he said.

He turned to Boyd and Bickers, and said, "I think we now understand the problem here."

Bickers replied, "And there are miles and miles of Roland land all along this river. How are we ever goin' to know where they will hit next. We just lucked into them today. Now what?"

"Good question," Sullivan replied. "Some of you Boys go round up the mules."

Four Rangers got back on their horses and went after the mules.

"Ya know," said Boyd, "they been skinning them over here a lot according to what we saw. But this time they took them to Mexico. Wonder why? What's the difference this time."

"We are," Sullivan answered. "We're the difference."

"You thinking what I'm thinking?" Bickers asked.

"Yep," Sullivan replied, as he spit in the river. "Somebody saw us and knew who we were. Told the Mexicans, or maybe some of them just figured us out right quick. Those we saw in the cafe might have seen us looking at them and figured out something was up."

"Well, they're on to us now," Boyd said.

"Our secret is out."

"Who is that comin' yonder?" asked Billy Smith.

They all turned around and saw riders coming toward them. They were riding fast, stirring up a rolling cloud of dust.

"Must be Roland's men," Bickers said.

"Yep," Sullivan answered.

The group of wranglers pulled up to the river, dismounted, and began watering their horses.

"Hey," one of them said, walking over to Sullivan, Boyd, and Bickers. "I'm Sandy Cook. We heard the shooting. Y'all the Rangers, I guess."

"We are," Sullivan replied. "Toombs Sullivan. William Boyd and Sam Bickers."

"Glad you're here. Hope you can do what we've not been able to do. Stop them."

"We'll try. But we did not stop them today. They were too smart for us. We think they already figured out who we are. Saw us in town last night. Sorry we didn't help ya none."

"You couldn't help that. You all might as well stay out here with us so you'll be where it all takes place. We got several cabins where we stay, back up a few miles. The food ain't that great. But it's eatable."

"Sounds fine with us. Lead us on."

As they rode along behind the cowboys, Sullivan looked over at Boyd.

"Now we gonna find out why we are Rangers and not cattle drovers like these boys."

"I already know why. I can't see looking at the rear ends of cows all day. Ridin' over what they do, steppin' in it, smellin' it all day. Cows just stink. Worse than horses."

"Yeah. And I don't guess the accomadations are all that wonderful. Can you imagine what livin' out here all the time is like? No wonder when they go to town, they go crazy. And I have seen it. In Fort Worth. And I do mean crazy, Boyd."

"I'll take yore word for it. I can kind of understand it. In a way, ya know."

"I know. But still I didn't put up with it. I banged'em on top of the head and put'em in jail for the night."

"What did they say to ya the next mornin'?"

"They didn't remember nothin'. Didn't know who I was or where they were. Had no idea they spent the night in jail till I opened the cell and led them out on the street."

"That' just crazy."

"We better hurry along. We're laggin' behind a little."

Chapter 21

There were four cabins for the cattle wranglers down on that part of the ranch. Each cabin had 10 bunks. There was a fifth building which was the kitchen and dining area.

The Rangers were put in cabins three and four. They took in their gear and selected their bunks.

That evening a meal was served which was steak, beans, biscuits, gravy, and coffee.

As they sat at the long tables, Sandy Cook was across from Sullivan.

"We eat a lot of steak, as you can see and imagine. But it's not the same at every meal. Tonight, we're eatin' steak, beans, and biscuits. Probably tomorrow it'll be beans, biscuits, and steak. Then the next night I'm guessin' biscuits, beans, gravy, and steak.

Now breakfast is different. That'll be eggs, bacon, biscuits, gravy, and steak. And coffee at every meal. Always coffee. That never changes like the other items do."

"Good to know," Sullivan replied with a smile. "Tell me, you boys been at this very long? Herding these cows around?"

"It varies. Some of us been here a good while, a few years. Others have come along one at a time. Most of us grew up around cattle, came from small ranches or farms. Some of us, uh, been running from the law, if ya don't mind me saying so, and wound up here at the bottom tip of Texas."

"Well, relax. We ain't here lookin' for none of you."

"What's yore plan gonna be?"

"I don't rightly know yet. Not sure how we'll know when they gonna hit next and where."

"Yeah, that's one of the problems we faced. Course, we ain't exactly prepared to fight an army which is about what they are, former soldiers and all."

"We'll have to figger it out as we go along, I guess. Got to be some way to

know where they're gonna to be."

"Mister Roland said you Rangers could stop this if anybody can. He also said if y'all can't stop it, then nobody can and there ain't nothing that can be done."

"That's a big responsibility, but that's what we were sent here to do."

"I hope you can. It's been a long day. Me and the boys'll be turning in now. Sleep tight, and if ya need anything, just figger it out for yoreself. We probably can't help ya."

The wranglers got up and left. The kitchen help came in to clear the tables.

Sullivan gathered the Rangers all around a couple of the tables.

"Well, I guess you heard most of what we were sayin'."

Bickers replied, "Yep. So what ya think we might be able to do?"

"Not sure I know yet. You saw today how it is, what we're up against here. There ain't no way we can stop them like we was tryin' to today. I don't know how we can get to where they are before they start movin' cattle. The best and most ideal thing would be to catch them as they come across the river, but how can we ever do that? Guess we could just go out on patrol. Split up into two groups, look for smoke from fires. Don't fire shots to make a signal, but send messengers if we find them. We'll just have to depend on luck. But neither group should go after them alone. Just wait on the other to arrive. Neither group is strong enough to take them on, I don't think. How's all that sound to ya?"

The men all nodded their heads in agreement. Both Bickers and Boyd said, "Good."

"All right. We'll get an early start in the morning. Boyd with me. Bickers leads the other group. You two decide how to divide up the men. Select who you want. Don't matter to me. Let's get some sleep. If we can."

The Rangers got up from the tables and made their way to the two bunk houses they were given.

Soon the lights were turned out as they all attempted to sleep. At least they could rest.

Sullivan had a difficult time falling asleep, as usual. Some of the men could turn off their brains, clear their minds, and drift away fairly quickly.

Not so with Sullivan. He had too much stuffed inside his brain. Everything in there competed for his attention. They all bounced off each other causing his eyes to be wide open. There had been too many adventures, too much killing, too many trips out into dangerous country, too many Indians, too many robbers, killers, highwaymen, too much law, and two much order. Two wives lost, two too many, one wife found again and lost again. A son lost, one too many. An unborn child lost, one too many. Too many friends lost, killed by savages, buried out in the most god-awful places, their graves grown over, sand and dirt blown over them with no one ever knowing where they lay, not even him now. And there were too many bullets fired by him into too many Indians, too many robbers, too much killing by him, too many fights.

And here he was, still at it. Just doing what he had been doing as though he was used to it, did not mind it, frankly rather enjoyed it, lived for it, could not live without it, wanted to keep doing it.

Well, he thought, that must be true. That must really be the case. He could not imagine trying to live without all this. He could not live a normal life, whatever that was, because he was no normal man. And he knew it. No, there was something that kept him at it, kept him searching, going after whoever it was he had been assigned to bring to justice, to their death, to their graves. His attempts to settle down had not been successful. So why fight it any more, why try to do anything other than what he was doing?

He was well suited for all this. He knew it. He was suited for nothing else. He enjoyed killing. He enjoyed hating. He enjoyed killing with a perfect hatred. He was good at it.

Somewhere in the night he drifted away into that land of rest and sleep and peace, except that sometime there was no peace. His dreams were so often filled with all the things that filled his mind.

Early the next morning he rousted everyone out of bed.

"Sleep well?" asked Boyd.

"Not hardly," Sullivan replied.

Chapter 22

"All right," said Sullivan, "we'll follow the river west. Bickers you take yore men and go along even with us, but maybe a mile or more north of us. Remember, no shots fired unless ya have to. Just send somebody to get us if ya see them. Let's get at it."

The day was hot already. It would be hot and dusty, a day not fit to be out in it, yet they were used to that, if a man can get used to being almost overcome by the heat, a dry parched throat, never enough water to drink, difficult on the horses as well. But they all knew not to complain, for complaining amounted to nothing when there was nothing to be done. Just be glad to be alive and hope to be when the day is done.

The two groups of Rangers headed down toward the river. After a couple of miles, Bickers headed off west as Sullivan and his men went on to the river. Once they reached it, they turned up along its banks headed to the west.

While Sullivan saw plenty of cattle, there was no sign of any rustlers. It was the same with Bickers and his group.

Both groups moved slowly along, keeping their eyes wide open, and not wanting to ride up on someone and alarm them.

After almost an hour, Sullivan saw a rider coming their way. It was Billy Dunnagan.

He exclaimed as he got near, "Sullivan! They're already driving cows toward the river to cross it! About a mile further up we think!"

"Tell Bickers to fire on them! We'll try to head 'em off! Let's go, Men!"

Dunnagan turned around and headed back to Bickers!

Sullivan and his men raced along the river!

Could they get there in time?

Could they head them off?

How many of them?

How many cows?

In minutes, they saw the dust coming beyond a rise!

It was them all right!

Sullivan pulled out his pistol as did the others!

"Get ready!"

Over the rise came the wild herd running for the river!

Shots were being fired by the Mexican rustlers!

"Let 'em have it!" Sullivan shouted, as he rode toward the herd and the Mexicans!

His Rangers followed him firing shots also!

They hit only a couple of the rustlers. The shots they fired only caused the cattle to move faster toward the river.

Now they were hearing other shots off to the right coming closer! It was Bickers and his men.

The Mexicans were returning fire at both groups of Rangers and hitting nobody, but they did not seem to mind. Their job was to get the cattle across the river.

Cows and dust and horses and Mexicans all went wildly into the river! They were across it in no time, at least three to four hundred cows. The Mexicans never looked back.

Bickers was there now. He and his men joined in firing at the Mexicans, missing all of them.

The Rangers sat on their horses, the shooting was over, as they watched the herd and the thieves disappear. They were all speechless for a few moments.

"Would ya look at that," Boyd said, as he pushed his hat back up off his forehead.

"I'm looking," replied Bickers.

"Don't look like there's no way of stoppin'em," added Ben Warner.

Then Sullivan spoke.

"I think we're beginning to understand the problem with this situation. Water yore horses. Take a bath in this fine river if ya like. A good opportunity."

The Rangers dismounted, and led their horses to the edge of the river. When the horses had their fill, the men began to undress. Then they went in the river, most of them sitting down in it. Once they were through bathing, they sat down along the banks to dry off. Several conversations were begun in the several small groups of the men.

"I'll say one thing," Boyd commented.

"Say it," replied Bickers.

"This is one well organized operation. That General Vega, De Vega, whoever he is, really knows what he's doin'. Him being a general and all, he knew just how to set this up and get it done. Them Mexicans we are seein'. They ain't no cow thieves. They are soldiers, cow soldiers. They follow orders. He sends them out to do battle, and they win. Every time. They win."

"Thought you was goin' to say one thing," Bickers responded. "You said a bunch of things. But I got to say, you are right. So right."

"How will we ever stop them?" Boyd asked.

"I have no idea," Sullivan replied.

"Got to be some way," Bickers said.

"Got to be," Sullivan answered. "Well, let's head on back and have some steak and beans."

"And biscuits," Boyd suggested.

"Yeah. Don't forget the biscuits," responded Bickers.

All the way back to the cabins, Sullivan was silent. He wondered over and over about Boyd's question. He hated to admit what he said was true. He had no idea about what to do. The only way would be waiting at the river when they first came across, but how would they ever know where that would be? If they spread out far enough so they could cover a lot of it, then that would be dangerous for one or two men who could never stop them, nor defeat them. They would not have time to signal for help. The help that showed up would find them dead.

Sullivan was led to what was possibly the only thing to do. It was not legal. If he tried that, he could be kicked out of the Rangers or maybe put in jail. That is if he even lived to tell what he had done. But there seemed to be no other way.

The day would be fading now, a day wasted in a way. It was afternoon. The heat was at its height. Though all of the men had bathed in the river and dried in the sun, they were all now wet again, wet with sweat.

As they drew near the cabins where the wranglers stayed, Sullivan looked ahead and saw one man standing there. He was by himself waiting on them.

It was Roland.

Sullivan knew he would want a good report, something positive, some progress, something.

He had nothing at all. No good report, nothing positive, no progress, nothing, nothing he could share with a man who wanted something, anything.

Truth be known, Sullivan had no idea of what to do to stop all this thievery. In all his years as a Ranger, he had never faced any situation like this one. He had chased Indians and crooks all over parts of Texas. He had out-witted, out-ridden, out-shot, out-killed, out-foxed them all. Now what?

Chapter 23

"Come on in," said Roland. "The cooks have a fine meal waiting on us."

"Let me guess what it is," Sullivan said, as he got down off his horse. "We'll wash up and be right along."

The Rangers put their horses in the barn, put away their saddles and gear. Then they went outside the building where the kitchen was, and began trying to wash the dust and sweat off their faces and hands. They took their hats off and beat them against their pants, and stomped their feet.

Roland greeted them when they went inside, "Welcome, Men, have a seat, have a seat. Food will be right out."

They sat down at the long tables, Roland across from Sullivan.

Soon the food came out and was served. It was the standard meal, but the men had not eaten all day. So it was wonderful to them. They ate as usual with great gusto.

Roland asked Sullivan a question.

"Well, how is it going?"

"You mean have we had any success?"

"Yes, success."

"No success, so it is not goin' good so far."

"I know it is difficult."

"Difficult? It's impossible. What we are trying to do just will not work. I can see that already."

"How you mean?"

"We have no idea where they gonna hit. By the time we find out, they're on the way to the river with your cattle. By then, it's too late. We can't stop'em. That's what happened today. We killed a couple of his men. They killed none of ours. And maybe four hundred of your cows are being killed right now."

"So what are you thinking?"

"I been thinking."

"A little more expressive perhaps?"

"I'm thinking we got to get this De Vega."

"Get him? How?" Roland asked.

"We can't get him here, right?"

"He never comes across the river. Well, he does sometime, but few see him. He has been seen, but his appearances are not predictable."

"So anybody who wants to get him has to go across the river."

"Is that legal?"

"No."

"It's another country."

"Yep. Mexico."

"Then, how can you?"

"Sometime you have to break the law in order to enforce it."

"Mister Sullivan, how can you get away with that?"

"I have broken it before. Would not be the first time I went into Mexico to get somebody."

"There's no telling how many men he has down there at his place. You think your men can go up against his, what amounts to, an army? On his own land?"

"No. There's not enough of us for that. Twenty men can't get in there. It would be suicide. But one man just might can get in there and kill him."

"Are you serious?"

"Dead serious."

"I don't like the way you put that . . . . dead serious."

"How about seriously dead?"

Roland smiled and thought for a moment.

"I asked for results. You are in charge of that department."

"What do you know about his place?"

"From what I hear and understand, he has a rather large settlement over there, not too far away I don't think. There is his big house and a good many other smaller houses where his men live. I have never seen it of course, but you can expect a wall around his house. It could be difficult getting in there."

"I would expect it would be difficult. And I would think well guarded. That's why one man could slip in there when it's dark and get him."

"You said could."

"Yes. That one man could also be killed," said Sullivan with a wry smile.

Nothing was said for a little while as both men ate and pondered what Sullivan had stated. Roland was thinking Sullivan was out of his mind. Sullivan was thinking the same thing about himself.

"Well," Roland finally said, "if you think that's the only way, then have at it. I want results. I can't tell you how to get them."

"It's all I know to do at this point."

When everyone had finished eating, Sullivan tapped his spoon on his coffee cup. He stood up and spoke.

"Listen up, Men. I've come to a decision without asking for yore opinion because I knew what it would be. What we tried to do today did not work. It ain't never gonna work. All we'd be doin' is wearing out horses and wasting ammunition. I've come up with a better idea. The key to this thing is to get the head man. He ain't never comin' over here at a time when we would know it, so somebody has got to go get him. The head of that snake, De Vega, has got to be cut off. We all can't get in there. It's the job of only one man. Alone. I am that man. I'm goin' over there and find him and kill him. Then I'm comin' back here where you'll be waitin' on me and we goin' back up to Austin."

The room was dead silent. It was like no one was even breathing.

After a few moments, that seemed like hours, Bickers was the first to speak.

"I say no to that idea. You don't stand a chance. You'll never come back out of there."

"I agree," added Boyd. "I think we all agree. You can't do that. We can't let you do that."

"You noticed I did not ask for any opinions. I did not put this up to a vote. I'm goin' over the river. I may be fired if I make it back. I don't want that to happen to y'all, Bickers, you're in charge till I get back. I'm leavin' in the morning. Now see to yore horses and then get some rest."

Chapter 24

"Sullivan," said Roland, early the next morning, "this is Anton Maldanado. I know you want to go alone, but you'll be lost over there if you don't know where you're going. He speaks good English. He grew up not far from De Vega's hacienda. He knows right where it is. I urge you to take him with you."

Sullivan looked at Roland, then looked at Maldanado, then looked back at Roland. He then turned to Maldanado.

"You speak good English?"

"I do."

"You know where I need to go?"

"I do."

"You got your horse and stuff ready to go?"

"I do."

"Can you say anything other than I do?"

"I can."

"All right, go get yore horse and stuff, and catch up with me."

Then he said to Roland, "Thanks. I hope."

And to the other Rangers, "So long, Boys."

"Good luck."

"Be careful."

"Keep yore eyes wide open."

Sullivan got on his horse and rode off toward the river and Mexico.

Fifteen minutes later, Maldanado was closing fast on him. Sullivan stopped to let him catch up.

Soon they came to the river. They stopped to let the horses drink. When they had their fill, Sullivan looked at Maldanado.

"Well, this is it."

"Si."

"Let's get over there. No time like right now."

They eased their horses down into the river and went slowly across. When they came out on the other side, they stopped for a moment and looked around.

Sullivan thought, well, yes, this really is it. This is Mexico, and I have done it now. I hope this is worth it. I hope it is worth being kicked out of the Rangers. But we were told what to do. We were not told what not to do. Nobody told me do not go into Mexico. So here I am for good or ill. But I hope I am not here for good as in being dead in the ground, and I hope it ain't for ill as in it don't go well.

"How far we got to go?" he asked Maldanado.

"Oh, maybe thirty mile from here. Maybe more."

"All right. Lead out."

Maldanado gently kicked his horse in the ribs and moved on ahead. Sullivan fell in behind him.

The land was barren looking, desert like, but there were some small trees and scrub and shrubs. And hot. The land was hot. Everything looked hot. Sullivan thought Texas was hot, but it was Mexico this time of the year that defined hot.

There was no water anywhere to be seen, but Sullivan knew there was water somewhere because people and trees and cattle cannot survive without water. Maldanado would know where the water was. He hoped.

Sullivan looked up and saw buzzards circling above not too far away. That could only mean one thing, well, two things he said to himself. It's either a dead man, a bad sign, or a place where there were many carcasses of cattle, another bad sign. There was never anything good about buzzards circling in the sky.

Maldanado stopped and held up his hand. He said nothing, and did not turn around and look at Sullivan. Sullivan did not move, nor did he say anything, ask anything. He waited.

"Stay here," Maldanado then said, as he turned halfway around in his saddle. He slowly moved on ahead, taking it very slow and very easy. He soon disappeared beyond the scrub and small trees. In moments he came back.

"A place where they killed the cows. A bad sight. Come on."

Sullivan followed Maldanado for several hundred yards. Then the odor became stronger and stronger. There was no doubt about what lay ahead. Soon they saw them. Several hundred dead cows left to rot in the sun and be consumed by the buzzards and animals. Buzzards were hopping all over the cows, helping themselves to fine meals. Stripped skins lay everywhere, hundreds in piles and off by themselves.

They stopped at the edge of this open ground of death, this killing ground, skinning grounds, rotting ground.

Maldanado looked over at Sullivan, held up his right hand, and rubbed his thumb against his index finger, signifying the rubbing together of coins, lots and lots of money. Sullivan nodded his head.

Then Maldanado said, "Mister Toombs, we move on away from here. I know a good place for us to camp and plan what is next."

They both knew what was next. But it was the details that might be the problem. Always the details, the place where the devil lived.

After they had ridden several more miles, they came to a good place to stop. There was shade, firewood, and a creek. They watered their horses, gathered wood, and started a fire.

Maldanado began preparing food he had brought, beans, peppers, tomatoes, onions, and dried beef.

Sullivan sat on a stump and watched him, and said, "Toombs. No Mister Toombs."

"Mister Toombs, I mean, Toombs, this man De Vega is a very smart man. He is shrewd. His men are very loyal to him. He rewards them very well. He pays them good. Some of them have families there where we are going. Others do not, but there are women for them. And De Vega has women, more than one I am told. His men will kill for him. Anyone they will kill. And they will die for him. To protect him they will die."

"Sounds like he thinks of everything."

"He thinks of everything."

"You think I can get in there?"

"You think you can. That why we are here. What you think is what matters. That will get you in."

"You think I can get out?"

"I hoping so. It is can we get out. I better go all the way and hold the horses outside so you can get away if you get back outside."

"What kind of chance do you think I have?"

"A good one. We eat now."

It was still hot as the sun was going down and would be for several hours.

As usual, Sullivan stayed awake a long time thinking about the next day, what might happen, what might not happen, and wondering why he was there and why was he doing this. But he knew.

Chapter 25

"Mister Sullivan," Maldanado said, as he and Sullivan sat by the fire drinking coffee.

"It's Toombs."

"Mister Toombs."

"Just Toombs. No Mister."

"Did you sleep well?"

"I slept some. You?"

"Very well. Toombs, I have a suggestion. If you would like one that is."

"I would like a suggestion."

"If anyone sees you dressed the way you are, you will be killed pronto."

"You think so?"

"No. I do not think so. I know so. I know this place and the people who live around here. Few good people here in this place, mostly the bad, like the General De Vega and his men. And lots of the bandits who like to kill anybody for the little money they might have on them."

"So what is your suggestion?"

"We get you in some different clothes so you look like me and not like you. You look like a Gringo. You need to look Mexican."

"Sorry. I brought nothing else with me."

"I take care of that. I have a brother not too far from here. He live in the place where there are some farmers and shepherds and a church. The bad stay away from there and leave them alone. We go to his house and get some clothes like we all wear. This will help the chance you have."

"That's a good suggestion."

That morning, Sullivan and Maldanado rode almost twenty miles to a small village. They passed by crops of corn and sugar cane. There were a number of cows and goats in pens. There were nine or ten small houses and a church in the middle of the village. When they arrived at the last house on the right, they stopped and dismounted. A man came out of the house.

"This is my brother Fernando," Maldanado said, with a big smile. "And here is his wife, Maria."

Sullivan smiled and took off his hat.

"We need to speak English so my friend will understand."

"Anton! What bring you here? Yes, yes, English for the Gringo."

"This is Toombs Sullivan. He is a Texas Ranger. He is here on a special mission."

"Mission?"

"A job. A work he has to do."

"Si."

"We have a favor to ask of you."

"Favor. Si."

"He needs to be dressed like one of us. Uh, clothes like we wear."

"Oh, si."

"Hat. Shirt. Pants."

Fernando nodded his head and held up one finger signifying one minute. He came right back with a brown sombrero, a white shirt, and white pants. He handed the items to Sullivan with a big smile.

"I will pay you for these. How much?"

"No, no," Fernando replied. "A favor. We are honored to have you here in our home. What we have is yours. A friend of my brother is a friend to us."

"Well, thanks."

"Fernando, Maria, we need a place where we can talk. Uh, make plans."

"Si," she answered. "Come out back. I will prepare food for you."

Sullivan and Maldanado followed her around the house. Attached to the back of the house was a canvas awning with a table and chairs underneath it.

"Sit." she said. "I will be a moment."

They sat down at the table across from each other.

A few chickens ran around behind the house. An old dog was lying in the shade. He looked up, but as soon as he saw them, he laid his head back down and went back to sleep.

Two small boys peeped out the back door at them. As soon as Sullivan noticed them, they ducked back inside.

"What is your plan?" Maldanado asked.

"I think I need to see the place. Maybe I could slip in there at night, but I don't want to go in there blind. I need to know where everything is ahead of time."

"It is not really far from here. After we eat, we could go over and have a look, but not too up close. Be very dangerous to get close."

A few moments later, Maria brought out two plates which had on them enchiladas and beans, peppers, onions, and tomatoes. The enchiladas contained some kind of shredded meat and sauce. She went back inside, and then came back with a bottle of wine and two cups.

"Thank you so much," Sullivan said, as he looked up at her.

She smiled, nodded her head, and then went back in the house.

"There is a hill overlooking De Vega's hacienda. It is maybe five, six, seven hundred yards away. We could go there and get a good look. The whole place is like a village, like this one, only bigger. Lots of houses, barns, corrals. His men and their families live there. And there is a church there down on the far end."

"Soon as we eat, we go," Sullivan said, as he drank from the cup.

"Good."

"Is his place heavily guarded?"

"I don't think I would say it is heavily guarded. There are guards, but not that many. For you see, no one would go there who means any harm to anyone there. So lot of guards not needed. There will be a few out front, two, three. I would say maybe one or none in the back courtyard. You will see the whole place is surrounded by a wall to keep people out."

"How high is the wall?"

"Maybe ten feet."

"Do you know anyone there?"

"Not many. A few I grew up with went to join the General, for you see, they had no way to feed their families. They were good men. But not good now. They would kill anyone. They had never been killers before."

"Sometime a man will do anything to take care of his family. I have seen it. Then there are those who will do anything because of the meanness that is in them. They will rob, steal, and kill. They don't need a reason. They just do it. Some of them enjoy killin'."

"Si. The General, he got that kind as well. Maybe most of them are like that. They would love to kill you. Why? Because you are Texas. And the General, he would love to get his hands on you. It is all about losing Texas to the Gringos. He never got over that.

You are Texas to him."

"Let's make sure he does not get his hands on me or you."

"Si."

Chapter 26

"How do I look?" Sullivan asked, as he came out the front door wearing his new clothes and sombrero.

"You look like me!" Maldanado exclaimed.

"Wonderful. Wonderful," said his brother Fernando.

Maria did not say anything, as she held her right hand up to her mouth and laughed.

"Well, I'll give it a try," Sullivan replied, smiling.

"Ready to go?" Maldanado asked.

"No. But we're goin' anyway."

They mounted up and rode on out the end of the village, headed west.

As they faced the afternoon sun, Sullivan pulled his sombrero down over his face as much as he could. It was wider than his own hat, and seemed to help some. But the heat was relentless. Looking out in the distance, Sullivan saw the waves of it rising from the steaming earth.

Sweat was pouring off both of them. Now and then, Sullivan reached up one arm or the other and wiped on his sleeve the sweat from around his mouth.

The horses were feeling the heat also, even though they were not moving very fast.

Over an hour later, they came to a place where Maldanado held up his hand, signaling they should stop.

"See that hill out there off to the right. That is where we need to go for a good sight."

Sullivan nodded his head, as they veered off toward the hill. When they reached it, they got down off their horses and led them up the hill. It was two to three hundred feet high, but not steep at all. Neither the men nor the horses had any trouble climbing it.

Once they were there, Sullivan took his binoculars from his saddle bag and looked across at the village.

"What you see?" asked Maldanado.

"Chickens," Sullivan replied, as he handed the binoculars to Maldanado.

"Si. I see. And goats. And a few cows for milk, and . . . . look like beef to eat also."

"We know they are well fed. And we know where those cows came from. Roland cows, I'd be willin' to bet."

"Si."

Maldanado handed the binoculars back to Sullivan, who looked through them again.

"There's that wall around that hacienda."

"A detail I am glad I tell you about. A surprise would not be good."

"Speaking of detail . . . . I cannot tell much about it. I just see the wall, and the roofs. A large house, and some smaller buildings it looks like."

Sullivan spent a few minutes looking all around the village and all the houses and barns.

"You ever been in that village?"

"Me? Never. Not anyone I ever knew that went in and lived to come back out. You do not go in there."

"I think I will."

"You mean now?"

"Right now."

"No. Don't go."

"You stay here."

"No. I go with you, but not a good idea. But you should not go alone. Worse idea."

"I got to go in and see what that place is all about. If I just wait until dark, I will have no idea where I am and where to go."

"I understand that, but this is still not a good idea. You might not live to see tonight or go in after dark. Not at all. No."

"Come on," Sullivan said, as he turned his horse around and started back down the hill.

Maldanado followed him, but he was not happy about it.

When they mounted up, they rode slowly toward the village.

"Keep your head bent down," Maldanado said, "like you are about half asleep. That way maybe they don't see your white face."

"Right."

As they approached the village, no one seemed to notice them. Chickens ran free around houses and across the only street. Now and then a dog would chase one. Other dogs lay asleep in what shade they could find, not caring anything at all about chickens.

They heard a dog bark, and another answered him beyond the houses. There was the steady beat of a hammer on metal at a blacksmith's shop. The voices of a few children playing in a yard behind a house caught their attention for a moment.

As they rode by the hacienda, they saw an armed guard standing by the gate. He did not seem to notice them.

When they came to the church, Sullivan suddenly stopped. He pointed at it.

"The bell tower," he said.

They got off their horses in front of the church, and then led them to a small tree off to the right. They tied their reins.

"What are we doing, Mister Sullivan?"

"No Mister."

"But what?"

"Follow me."

"Hail Mary, Mother of God," Maldanado said, as he crossed himself three times.

When they got to the front door, they opened it slowly, stepped inside, and looked around. There was no priest to be seen.

"He is probably asleep," Maldanao whisperd. "Let's not wake him."

Sullivan pointed to the stairs of the tower. They began slowly climbing up them. They moved softly, trying not to make any noise, stepping lightly.

When they reached the top, they looked out over the grounds of the hacienda.

"Well, there it is. Look at that back wall. I'm thinking that would be the best place for me to get in. Just climb over it . . . . somehow."

"I thinking that would be as good a place to die as any."

"Let's hope not. Think his bedroom is upstairs?"

"Why not?"

"There might be a way to climb up there. Otherwise, I'll have to go in the lower floor, and then find the stairs."

"He may have a guard inside the house."

"Good idea. I'll be careful about that."

"Let's get out of here."

"All right."

"When we reach the horses, we go around the church and take a right. Not go back up the street."

"Good thinkin'. That'll give me a look at the back of that place. I want to know everything about it ahead of time."

"I thought you were a brave Gringo. Now I am thinking you are crazy."

"I think you just may be right about that. Only a crazy man would attempt such a stunt as this. But it's what I came down here to do. Put a stop to the cow thieves. The General is the head cow thief. So I will put a stop to him. A permanent one."

They quietly slipped back down the stairs, taking small steps one at a time, hoping they would not wake up the sleeping priest.

They went outside, untied their horses, and got on them. They slowly rode off to the right and circled around behind the village.

They went along beside the back wall of the hacienda. Sullivan looked closely at it. He looked up and down the wall trying to judge the height of it.

He said softly, "Yep. About ten feet."

On the way back to the Maldanado house, Sullivan thought about what he would do and how. He would wait until it was very dark, then not go in until after mid-night. He would wear his own clothes. The white shirt and pants were too easy to see in the dark and what light might fall on him. That was the plan. It might even work.

All the way back to the other village, Sullivan kept thinking about his plan. He had to admit to himself it was just a little bit crazy. But it was too late to come up with any other idea. He was there. The general was there. He was committed.

When they arrived at Maldanado's brother's house, Maria had another meal ready for them. It was much the same as the one earlier.

They sat down at the same table. The same old dog looked up at them. This time he got up and wandered off. The same little children peeped out the door at them, and then disappeared quickly.

Sullivan picked up his cup and drank the same wine.

Chapter 27

Sullivan and Maldanado rode through the dark night. All along the way, Sullivan kept thinking about what was about to happen, what he was going to do. At least he was going to try to do it. He began having misgivings about the whole thing. How did he ever come up with such an idea? Yet he was convinced there was no other way. There was nothing else he could do, so he would just follow through with the plan.

He felt the hot night air blowing across his face. Does it ever cool down here? He wondered. He was sweating some, not much, but a little. Was it the heat or was it his nerves? He did not know and did not really care.

They came near the village and saw the hill off to their right. They got off their horses and led them up the hill. Standing on the hill, they watched the village. They saw many lights go out as the people there went to bed. There were still lights at the hacienda. These were in the front courtyard they thought. But Sullivan would go over the wall in the back, so these would probably not reveal him. He hoped.

It was well past mid-night now. It was time to go.

"Well, this is it," Sullivan said.

"If you say so."

"I did."

"I don't like it."

"I don't either, but this is what I came down here to do."

They slipped back down the hill and got on their horses. They rode slowly toward the back of the hacienda.

When they got there, they dismounted. Sullivan stood by his horse and looked up at the wall. He thought, yes it was at least ten feet tall. He looked at the wall and then at his horse. He looked over at Maldanado, then at the wall, and then at his horse.

"Here, hold my reins."

He got back on his horse, stood up on it, and then reached up, placed his hands and arms on top of the wall. He pulled himself up on the wall. Then he turned around and lowered himself down to the ground.

Once on the ground, he squatted down for a moment. He heard no one and saw no one. Lucky for him, there was not a guard in the back of the house.

Straight ahead beyond a patio and garden was the back wall of the large two-story house. He thought he could see the back door.

He looked carefully all across the back of the house and the patio area. There was still no guard anywhere that he could see.

He decided to make his move. Staying close to the ground, he hurried toward the back door. Once he reached it, he stood still, leaning against the wall just to the right of the door. Still there was no one around. There was no noise of any kind. All was quiet.

He put his hand on the knob, slowly turning it. The door was un-locked. He gently pushed it open.

There were no lamps or candles burning on the first floor. He stepped inside and stood still leaning against the right wall. He stood there barely breathing. He did not hear anyone moving around anywhere in the house. He was glad.

Then he thought, how will I get back over that wall without my horse or anything to stand on? Worry about that later. If I live through this, that is.

As he breathed in the air, he picked up the scents of peppers, onions, wine, and smoke, perhaps cigar smoke, he thought.

He saw he was standing in a wide central hall that ran the length of the house. He slowly moved along the hall, staying close to the wall. Now he could see there was a stairway half way up the hall. He slowly moved toward it.

He stood in the shadows, barely breathing still, not moving even a finger. He waited.

De Vega must be asleep up there, he said to himself. There must be a large bedroom up there on that floor. That would be his for sure. He would be up there for many reasons. Safety was one of them in case somebody came in at night and wanted to kill him.

Now Sullivan stood at the foot of the stairs. He looked up them. No lamps or candles burning up there either.

He kept wondering why there was no one else in the house. Why wasn't there at least one guard?

He put his right foot on the first step. There was no sound, no squeaking. This was good. Then with his left foot he touched the second step. Nothing. All was quiet. Good.

He slowly moved up the steps, carefully, quietly. No sounds. Nothing. Still good.

When he reached the top of the stairs, he stood still. He looked up and down the hall. He saw no one. No lights. Nothing.

He slowly moved toward the front of the house, thinking the biggest bedroom, De Vega's, must be that way. He would be up that way for sure.

He came to a closed door on the left. Other doors were open. This must be the one. He would have the door to his room shut for safety and privacy.

He slowly pushed the door open, having silently turned the knob.

It was not locked either. Why didn't people there lock their doors? It was too easy to get inside.

There were two people in a large bed. He could see them. His eyes had adjusted to the darkness enough for him to tell it was a man and a woman. They were not moving at all. They were sound asleep, he could tell from their breathing.

There was no cover over them. He moved closer. The young woman was naked. The man had on some kind of loose-fitting pants, no shirt.

Sullivan stood over them. He pulled out his pistol from under his belt. He pulled a knife from the inside of his left boot.

Which should he use? The pistol would bring men into the house and up the stairs before he could get down them or out of the house at least. The knife would be quiet of course, but there was the young woman. She would scream if she woke up. She was too beautiful to also kill. He did not kill women. He had never killed an Indian woman, even by mistake. Standing there with the knife, he quickly thought about what had been done to his wife. He wanted nothing to do with anything like that.

Could he kill De Vega without waking her up? Maybe he could just knock her out before she had a chance to make any noise. He would slice his throat open quickly, and then hit her on the head with his pistol. That would be better than shooting him, much better.

He chose the knife, and slipped the pistol back under his belt. He moved even closer to De Vega.

There he was sleeping so peacefully, unaware that he was about to meet his maker or his father, the devil himself. It did not matter to Sullivan which one it was. He would leave that to them. They could debate or fight over him. My job, he thought, is just to dispatch him. Right now.

Sullivan felt cold steel on the back of his neck. He did not move.

Chapter 28

"What are you doing, Gringo?" a voice behind Sullivan asked.

A lamp was lit as another of De Vega's men stood by a table with a match in one hand, and his other hand on the lamp. He blew out the match.

"What! Uh! What? What is it?" De Vega cried out.

The young woman screamed for a second and quickly found a sheet she pulled up over herself.

"General, we found this Gringo standing over you with the knife he has in his hand. Drop the knife, Gringo. What should we do with him? Take him outside and shoot him or slice him open like a pig with his own knife?"

"Ah . . . . let me get awake."

De Vega stood up, and then picked up a cup with some wine still in it. He drank from the cup. A little of the wine ran down both sides of his mouth to his chin.

"Gringo? So. What are you doing here, Gringo? In my house? By my bed? With a knife?"

De Vega looked Sullivan up and down.

"A gringo. In my house."

Sullivan looked De Vega up and down. He was not what he had imagined. He was tall, slim, but also muscular. He had a well-trimmed mustache and goatee, solid black. He might be fifty or older, Sullivan thought, but what did he care about all that?

"Who are you? Tell me quick before I cut your throat with your own knife."

"I'm Toombs Sullivan."

"Why are you here?"

"I'm a Texas Ranger."

"So why are you here?"

"I have come to kill you."

"Ha ha ha! You did not do a very good job of it."

"I was just a little slow."

De Vega looked carefully at Sullivan as though he was trying to figure him out.

"I have never seen a Texas Ranger before. I have heard of these Texas Rangers from friends of mine. But they do not think much of the Texas Rangers. And what is the reason for this so-called killing of me? Killing of me by the so-called Texas Rangers?"

"I'm doing it for the cows."

"The cows? What cows? You doing a favor for the cows? What do they care? What cows?"

"The ones you keep stealing off that big ranch in Texas. Roland's ranch."

"Did this Mister Roland, as you say, put you up to this?"

"No. The state of Texas put me up to it."

"The state of Texas said go kill General De Vega?"

"No. The state of Texas said go solve the problem. I came up with this idea on my own."

"On your own? Not a very good idea. And not carried out very well. If you were in my army, I would have you shot for being a case of total stupidity."

"I hesitated a little bit too long. I did not want to wake up your lady friend here."

"You would kill me for a few measly cows, and most of them look like they need killing very quick."

"They were not yours. It is against the law in Texas to steal another man's cows."

"Steal is not a very nice word. I prefer some other term. That man has thousands all over everywhere. I prefer a word like relief. I simply relieved him of some of his cows, thinned out his herd for him so others could fatten up better. And what do I care about the law of the state of Texas. This is Mexico. I live in Mexico. Things are done in a different way here in Mexico. And Texas Ranger, you are now in Mexico where you come under Mexico law and ways of doing things."

"You have stolen thousands of his cows so you can get rich off the tallow you send to Cuba. We know all about your operation."

"Si. You Gringos seem to have all the answers. Well, I would like to return to my sleep, and the young lady as well. I will not kill you now."

De Vega turned to his two men, and said, "Take our guest down to the cellar and tie him there. We will attend to him later."

"Gringo," one of them said, as he motioned toward the door with his head.

They took Sullivan down the stairs to the main floor, back down the hall where he had come in, and then they opened a door that led to the cellar.

"Down," one of them said, as the other one lit a lamp for them to see how to go down the stairs.

Sullivan went slowly down the steps with the two Mexicans right behind him.

They sat him down on the floor and tied his hands behind a post. They went back up the stairs taking the lamp with them, leaving him in the dark.

The cellar was dark and cool. It was the coolest place Sullivan had been in a long time.

Two minutes later, the door opened again. Sullivan heard footsteps on the stairs and the light was coming back down to the cellar.

"We brought you company, Gringo, so you will not be alone. Here is your friend."

They sat Maldanado down on the floor across from Sullivan, and tied him to a post.

"He was holding the horses. Not fast enough to jump on one and get away. Too bad, Gringo. No help coming for you."

When they left and went back up the stairs, Maldanado spoke first.

"Well, here we are."

"Sorry I got you into this mess. It didn't quite turn out the way I had planned. It seemed like a good idea at the time."

"Not your fault. It just is, that's all. But what went wrong?"

"I stood by his bed too long. I couldn't decide if I should shoot him or cut his throat. By the time I decided to cut his throat and knock his woman out if she woke up, his men came in the room behind me. They wanted to kill me then and there or take me outside and use my own knife on me. But for some reason De Vega did not let them do that. He sent me here to die later by what method I do not know."

"Bad luck, Sullivan, but never hesitate with a knife or a gun, especially with a knife. Be quick."

"Now you tell me."

"You should have asked."

"Maybe we can get out of here."

"I don't see how, Ranger Sullivan. I don't see at all in this dark."

"Yes. That is a problem."

"Big problem."

"Maybe they will bring us food at some point."

"Food? Who could eat it?"

"I'm not talking about eatin' it," Sullivan said.

"Then what you talk about?"

Chapter 29

Both Sullivan and Maldanado drifted in and out of half-sleep, too weary to stay awake, too uncomfortable to fall asleep.

They lost all track of time. They had no idea if it was still dark outside or if the sun had come up. They only knew they had been there a long time.

"Hey," Sullivan whispered.

"Mmmm."

"You awake?"

"I am now. Yes and no."

"I have an idea."

"Does it include staying asleep."

"No. It includes staying alive."

"Tell me, quick."

"Think they will bring us food?"

"I hope not."

"If and when, that will be our only chance."

"What are you thinking, or maybe what have you been drinking?"

"We can't eat tied up like this. They'll be two of them, I'm guessing.

They'll untie us so we can take the food from them. That will be our chance.

You fumble the plate any way you can. Get the attention of both. I'll jump both if I can, but you be quick to get one of them too."

"As good a way to die as any. I am not hungry anyway."

Another hour or two or longer passed. They could not tell how long. Sullivan kept looking in the direction of the stairs, though he could not see anything.

Finally, they heard a noise at the top of the stairs. The door opened slowly, letting in a little light. Then it swung wide.

A woman came down the steps carrying a tray. They could see her now. This made Sullivan's idea more complicated. Was it just her? Maybe that was good.

Then the same two men came down behind her, each with a lamp in his hand. Now it was more complicated again. But this had to work.

The woman sat the tray on a small table beside the wall, a table they had not noticed.

"I have brought you breakfast, Gringo," the woman said.

That meant it was day-time now, but what time Sullivan still had no idea.

The two men put the lamps down, one on the table, the other on the floor. This was it, their only chance.

Sullivan got ready. He was ready to pounce like a mountain lion. He only hoped that Maldanado was as well. He looked over at him, trying to look serious, trying to indicate this was it without giving away their plan.

The two men walked over behind Sullivan and Maldanado and began untying them. They drew their pistols and backed away.

"One wrong move, Gringo, and you do not eat the food. Why you getting food I do not know. I would rather just cut your throat right now,"

"Drop those pistols now! Before I kill you! Drop'em!"

In the dimly lit room, Sullivan and Maldanado saw William Boyd pointing his Winchester rifle at the two men.

"On the floor! You too, Woman!"

When Boyd looked at the woman, the two men turned to fire at him!

Bang!

Bang!

The men fell over on the floor!

The woman screamed!

"Shut up!" Boyd screamed back at her.

"Don't matter now, Boyd," said Sullivan. "The whole world heard those shots.

Let's get their guns."

Sullivan looked at the woman, "Get out of here!"

She looked puzzled. Does not speak English, Sullivan thought. He pointed to the stairs.

"Go!"

He and Maldanado took the pistols from the dead men and their belts. Sullivan put the pistol under his belt and flung the gun-belt over his shoulder.

He turned to Boyd, "Got horses?"

"Yours, his, mine."

"Grab that lamp," Sullivan said, pointing to the one on the table.

He picked up the one that was on the floor and threw it against a wall. The flames immediately began climbing the wall.

"Come on."

When they reached the top of the stairs, he looked out in the hall. No one was coming yet.

"Give me that lamp. Which way we go out?"

"The back," Boyd answered.

Sullivan ran up the hall and threw the lamp down at the bottom of the stairs to the second floor. He saw another lamp on a near-by table. He picked it up and threw it toward the front of the house.

"Let's get!"

Out the back door they ran across the patio toward the back wall. The thought, how can we get over it, ran quickly through Sullivan's mind.

Then he saw Boyd had found a ladder somewhere. It was waiting on them.

"You think of everything!"

"I aim to please!"

"Be prepared to aim that rifle well!" screamed Maldanado. "They will come! All of them!"

Sullivan turned back around facing the house as he yelled at the other two.

"Get up that ladder!"

Boyd motioned for Maldanado to go up first. He scampered up the ladder. Then he sat on the wall pointing his rifle back at the house.

"You two come on! I watch the house!"

Boyd quickly climbed up and over, jumping to the ground on the other side.

Then Sullivan did the same thing.

"Still clear!" Maldanado shouted, as he jumped down.

Chapter 30

Once over the wall they found the horses were waiting. They quickly mounted up and then Sullivan and Boyd turned to Maldanado.

"Which way?" Sullivan said to Maldanado.

"Head left to the west. We'll double back and throw them off. I hope."

"Me too."

Off they rode as fast as the horses could run. When they reached a rise a mile away, they stopped and looked back. The horses needed a few moments of rest.

They saw the dust rising far back behind them. It could only mean one thing.

"Here they come!" Boyd exclaimed.

"They wasted no time," answered Sullivan.

"We must not either," said Maldanado.

They kicked the horses and charged down off the rise.

They rode hard for several mile

s. Boyd then looked back again.

"They're still comin'!" he shouted. "I think they're gaining on us!"

"We can't do this all day!" responded Sullivan. "We'll kill these horses!"

"There!" shouted Maldanado.

They veered off to their tight, moving up onto a hill with large boulders in front of and all over it. It would be excellent cover. From there they could hold them off until they could think of something else or gain some advantage.

They jumped off their horses, Sullivan and Maldanado pulling their Winchesters off their horses all in one motion. Boyd was already firing his as the Mexicans came on toward them.

The three of them ducked behind large boulders as the Mexicans held up, splitting off to the left and right.

They fired at both groups!

Bang!

Bang!

Bang!

There were three already dead on the ground.

"That's three down!" Maldanado shouted.

"There must be over twenty of them!" Sullivan shouted.

"Who's counting?" Boyd replied.

"We need to kill more than three!"

"How about we kill them all?"

"Fine by me."

"There's one stickin' his head up," Boyd said.

Bang!

The head flipped backward.

"One more or one less, one less that is," Boyd said, with a slight smile.

"One fewer," Sullivan said.

"What? That's what I said."

"It's fewer, not less."

"You educated?" Boyd asked.

"No. Not at all, except what Mama taught me. She said fewer, not less."

"The ones to the left are now down in a long ditch. See?" Maldanado said. "And the others will circle around behind and up over us. They will pick us off."

"Like ticks off a dog. Three ticks. One dog," Boyd replied. "We'll be dead, more or less."

"Less alive. Shoot anything that moves. I'm going up the hill between the boulders to handle those who'll be up there," Sullivan replied.

Bang!

Bang!

Bang!

There shots rang out.

Three horses hit the ground, dead.

"Oh, hell! My favorite horse," said Boyd.

"My only horse," answered Sullivan.

"Si. My one horse," added Maldanado.

"What do we do now?" asked Boyd. "Three fewer horses. Not less."

"I'm goin' up this hill."

Sullivan stayed low to the ground as he made his way between the large imposing boulders, inching his way up the hill. He tried to stay down enough to keep from getting hit. But he had to get up that hill. It was a chance he had to take.

Bang ping!

Chips of stone flew around him!

Bang ping!

Bang ping!

Bang ping!

Well, they know where I am, Sullivan was thinking. What now?

Bang ping!

They're gonna keep on and one of those bullets is gonna bounce me up beside the head. I better put a stop to this.

Then he saw it, a clear path between larger boulders. The wide path led on toward the top of the hill. He could make it there without them ever seeing him. The boulders were large enough for him to be hidden as he made his way between them and up the hill.

He paused a moment, as he replaced in his Winchester the bullets he had fired earlier. Then he pulled the pistol he had gotten back in the basement from his belt. He checked it to see if it was fully loaded. It was.

Bang ping!

Bang ping!

Bang ping!

Those idiots think I'm still there in the same place, and they're hoping for a lucky shot if I should stick my head up. I don't think I'll be doing that.

Bang!

Bang!

Bang!

Boyd and Maldanado were keeping the others busy over on the other side.

They must have them pinned down in that ditch, Sullivan said to himself. Good. Good.

Just keep them there. Keep them pinned down.

Now, if I can make my way on up without gettin' myself killed, I can take out these up here. One at a time. But one at a time and they will know where I am, change where they are, and double back around on me.

Better think of somethin' else.

Chapter 31

Sullivan crawled around where he could see all nine of the Mexicans lined up side by side leaning against the large boulders. They kept firing where he had been.

Bang ping!

Bang ping!

Bang ping!

One at a time? No. No, that will never do. Six shots in the pistol. And the Winchester.

Suddenly he jumped up and ran down along behind the Mexicans firing the rifle, killing three with the Winchester, throwing it down, pulling out the pistol, and killing six more with it.

He drew fire from the others over in the ditch.

Bang ping!

Bang!

He quickly ducked down behind the boulders. What now? he thought.

He had to somehow get to where he could have a shot at them. Where they were and where Boyd and Maldanado were, this could go on all day and all night.

He crawled over to where the Winchester was and picked it up. Then he went back behind the boulders. He reloaded the pistol and put three bullets in the rifle.

There was silence as both sides stopped firing. It was useless. After a few minutes one of the Mexicans called out.

"Hey, Gringos! You two in front of us and you up the hill! Are you ready to give up? It is no use! You got no chance! Your horses are dead! We loved killing your horses. Where you are going you will not need no horses. Did you love your horses, Gringo cowboys? Too bad! What you gone do? Walk back to the river? It a good way off! You never make it!"

You killed my horse, Sullivan said to himself, as he jumped up and fired the rifle three times.

Bang!

Bang!

Bang!

"How many bullets you got, Gringo? You missed that time! You must be a very poor shot! I thought you Gringo cowboys could shoot!"

That's a good question. How many do I have? And Boyd and Maldanado?

"Maybe you better count them up!"

Sullivan knew he did not have many on him, only what was in his belt. There were plenty in his saddle bags on his horse, his dead horse, where he could not get to them.

But he had all of those belonging to the Mexicans he had just killed. So he was in good shape bullet wise. He did not know about Boyd and Maldanado, how many they had.

"This one's for you!" he shouted, as he jumped up and fired the rifle once.

Bang!

"You miss!"

Bang!

Bang!

Boyd and Maldanado fired, but they knew they would not hit anyone, hidden as they were behind the top of the ditch.

"You miss too, you other poor shot Gringo cowboys!"

"How many you got?" Boyd asked.

"Not enough," Maldanado answered.

"Maybe we better save what we got in case they rush us."

Yes, Sullivan thought, this could go on all day and all night. Maybe that's our only chance. Tonight. Tonight, I can get down to them. But, yeah, they can crawl right up to us as well.

Water would be nice, he was thinking. I have water in my canteen. It's on my horse, my dead horse. Maybe Boyd and Maldanado can get to theirs. I have to sit here the rest of the day without any. That's the least of my worries though. Wonder what time it is?

The long hot dry afternoon seemed like it would last forever. But as the day wore on, the sun moved on so that after a good while, Sullivan was in the shade behind the large boulders. That would help some.

The shadows became longer as the day was slipping away in the west. Soon it would be gone. Then it would be time to move. But he must wait for total darkness.

Even with the darkness, he would have to be very careful. The moon was full and bright, not a cloud in the sky.

Sullivan looked up at all the stars. He never grew tired of seeing them.

Time to move down, slowly, quietly, deliberately. He must not make a sound or rush this. He had waited all afternoon. A few more minutes would not hurt at all.

He crawled down to level ground. No one had seen him yet. Slowly he crawled over toward the ditch. This would be very dangerous. He did not know what it was like over there, how the ditch looked, where they would be.

This could be the end of the line. He had fought many battles, but this one could be the last one. But if he could kill most of them, then maybe Boyd and Maldanado could make it out of there and back across the river.

On he crawled, and as he did, the dust he stirred up found its way into his mouth. He was already dry enough, thirsty enough. This made it worse.

He crawled toward what he thought was the north end of the ditch. He could get down in it there, and then move along until he could see them. He would do the same thing as before – rush them firing the rifle and then up close, pull out the pistol.

He slid down in the ditch. He paused a moment to listen. He heard nothing. Maybe they were all asleep.

This would make it a lot easier, if they were sleeping, if he could surprise them, catch them off-guard.

Now he was about where they were. He stood up and ran toward them, ready to shoot them, ready to kill them, all of them.

He ran about thirty to forty yards and stopped. There was no one there.

He looked up over the top of the ditch and called out.

"Come on down here! They've gone!"

Boyd and Maldanado climbed down out of he rocks and came to where Sullivan was waiting on them at the ditch.

All three of them looked around, wondering what had happened to them, and where had they gone.

They began looking around for the horses of the ones Sullivan had killed. There were no horses to be found.

"They just ran off some place," Boyd said.

"Yeah," replied Sullivan. "Too bad we weren't on them."

Chapter 32

"They must have just left," Sullivan said.

"I didn't hear no horses leavin'," Boyd responded.

"Me neither," Maldanado added.

"Well," Sullivan then said, "I was countin' on killin' them and taking their horses or those of the ones I did kill. But we got no horses, Boys. We got a long walk back to the river."

"They will be coming after us at first light," Maldanado replied.

"Yeah" Sullivan said. "Course, we did not do yet what I came here to do."

"You mean the head of the snake thing?" Boyd asked.

"Yeah, that. Maybe we need to think this through a bit."

"Does that mean you already thought it through?"

"Right, Boyd. Just now as we speak. We're on foot now. We can get out ahead of them a good way. But they'll be coming after us at first light, yes, for sure, if not earlier. How long till they catch up with us? Out here in this country, we don't stand much of a chance."

"So you're suggesting what?"

"I don't know yet. Maybe we can get to a place where we can set up an ambush. Maybe we can get three of their horses. If so, and if we live through all that, I'm going back for the general. That's what I came here for, and I ain't givin' up. You two can go on across the river to Texas. Ya don't need to come with me."

Sullivan turned and began walking north. The other two fell in behind him.

The bright moon was above them so that they were able to see where they were going very well.

Sullivan looked up at the stars. He had always admired them for what they were, though he did not really know what they were, but they helped light up the sky. There must be a thousand up there he thought, maybe ten thousand. Who could count them? Nobody he knew. Besides he had no time for counting stars. Maybe there were more than ten thousand. There were a lot, he knew that.

He kept looking around trying to spot a good place for an ambush. He saw nothing. It was all flat land, no hills, no gulleys, just flat. This would never do.

Maybe they could make the river before dawn? No. It was too far away. But he knew before they got there, they would find the hills he was looking for, that is if they had time to get there.

Two hours later, they began to see the hills in the distance. They might still be a mile away or more, but it did not matter. They had time to get there.

Finally, they reached the hills. They climbed up into them and sat down to rest just off the often-traveled trail that led up into them.

"Boys, they will come right here. They will follow the trail to right here where we are."

"Is that good or bad?" Boyd asked.

"Good for us. Bad for them. I think."

"I hope you are right. I hope it's real bad for them and real good for us. That's means they are dead and we get horses."

"Boyd, what time is it?" Sullivan asked.

Boyd pulled his pocket watch out of his vest pocket and held it up in the moonlight so he could see it.

"Looks to be about three or so."

"Good. We got some time to catch some shut-eye."

"This was my Pa's watch. He gave it to me at the outbreak of the war. He said I would need it more than he would. He was right. I needed it, and he did not. He died before I got back home."

"Sorry, Boyd. At least you got that to remember him by. Life is so fragile. Ya don't know from one day to the next if ya gonna be here or not. Then the day comes when you ain't no more."

"Yeah. It came for him, and will for me. Mama died when I was fifteen. A cow kicked her in the head. Pa went out and shot the cow. We ate it."

On that somber note, they quieted down. They needed to rest and sleep if they could.

They laid back against the giant boulders, and all three were soon asleep.

Sullivan woke up as the first rays of sunlight slipped up over the hills. He looked around and wiped his eyes. He looked at his Winchester and made sure it was fully loaded. He missed having his Sharps with him. He needed that rifle. But it was up under his horse, his dead horse. The Winchester was faster anyway. He had to load the Sharps one bullet at a time. Maybe he could get it back later.

He watched Boyd and Maldanado as they continued to sleep. No need to wake them yet. It was still early, too early for their enemies to catch up to them. They would need all the rest they could get.

The sun was higher now and brighter. The other two began to stir around. Soon they were awake. They stood up and began stretching.

"No sign of'em yet?" Boyd said, as he yawned and reached his arms out to each side as far as he could.

"Not yet."

"Good. I need to get my bearin's a bit."

"I figure we can hold'em off right here, up in these rocks," Sullivan said. "Maybe the outcome this time will be different."

"I hope so. It's gonna get hot up in the day, and we ain't got no water."

"If they'll come on, we can get this over with and head for the river."

"Hope so. Hope over with is in our favor. If it's in their favor we won't need no water."

"At least we won't be dying of thirst."

"That's lookin' on the bright side," Boyd said, with a laugh.

The three men spread out among the boulders. They strained their eyes looking down toward the south, hoping to see anything that would indicate they were on their way.

It was almost nine o'clock now, the hours dragging by.

Sullivan kept looking. The sweat ran down his face. He wiped it away from his eyes and his mouth.

"Make every shot count," he said.

"Every one," Boyd replied.

"Si," called out Maldanado.

"You really think they're comin'?" asked Boyd.

"They're comin' for sure. Right Maldanado?"

"They are coming."

"Look," Sullivan said.

A small cloud of dust could be seen in the distance.

"What does that tell ya, Boyd?"

"They're comin'."

Chapter 33

"They won't see us up here," Sullivan said. "They'll think we went off to the river as fast we could or maybe still trying to get through these hills. They'll come charging up here wide open, as fast as their horses can run. Remember we need horses. Don't shoot any horses."

"Right," Boyd said, with a smile. "No horses."

With each moment, the small cloud of dust drew closer.

Soon the cloud of dust began revealing figures. Instead of a large group, they began seeing individual horses it seemed. Then they could see there were riders on them.

Now they were seeing colors, sombreros on tops of heads, light and dark shades of the horses.

"Get ready," Sullivan said, "but let'em get closer . . . . closer . . . . closer . . . .closer . . . . wait . . . . wait . . . . wait . . . . Now!"

Bang!

Bang!

Bang!

Bang!

Riders began falling to the ground!

Horses stumbled!

Horses got back up!

Horses began to run off in all directions!

Bang!

Bang!

Bang!

Bang!

The firing continued!

Some riders lay dead!

Others, wounded, tried to get up, some then fell over!

The Mexicans began firing back!

Some jumping down to the ground trying to hide behind dead hoses!

They died before they got there!

Others began to ride toward the Rangers!

They were shot dead off their horses!

Others tried to run back toward where they came from!

They never made it.

When the shooting was over, a few of the horses stood around. Other horses ran away. Four horses were accidently shot. They were dead.

There was no movement among the former riders of those horses.

Sullivan stood up and looked around.

"Let's go see what we got."

They walked back down the little trail. When they came to where the Mexicans lay dead, they began counting how many there where.

"Eighteen," Boyd said.

"Good," Sullivan replied. "Serves'em right."

Maldanado walked over to a horse and took his reins in his hand, and then the reins of two more. He led the horses to where Sullivan and Boyd stood among the dead Mexicans.

"While you two were counting dead Mexicans, I got us three live horses. I suggest we get on them and get out of here. Pronto."

"Good work," Sullivan said.

He looked at the other two men.

"Now you go on over the river. It ain't far now, I don't think."

"You ain't really going back right now, are ya?" Boyd asked.

"I reckon so."

"That ain't wise, Sullivan. Think a minute. I know I can't change yo mind once ya decide somethin'. But how about you change yo mind. Come on back with us. Rest a day. Re-equip ya-self. I'll come back with ya."

"Si. And me as well."

"Ya really think that is best?" Sullivan asked.

"Yep."

"Si."

"Aw-right. Y'all are like a couple of old women. But I'll do it. I don't like it, but I'll do it."

The three men mounted up on the borrowed Mexican horses and headed up over the hills and toward the river. They rode hard and fast, quickly putting distance between themselves and anyone else who might be wanting to catch up with them.

When they got to the river, they stopped to let the horses drink. They jumped down quickly and knelt by the water's edge where they could drink as well. They had been without water since the afternoon before. They took empty canteens from the horses and filled them.

Then they took off the gun belts they had gotten and their boots and hats and laid down in the water along the river's edge. The water was cool and refreshing and cleansing. Sullivan did not say anything about it, but every time he killed people like that, he felt like he needed to be cleaned off, cleansed of what he had done. It made him feel better about it.

After letting the horses and themselves rest for a few minutes, they mounted back up and went across the river.

Maldanado guided them to the cabins where they had stayed before.

Once they got there, they put the horses in a corral, washed up, and went inside to put their pistols and rifles up.

"I wonder if we can get any food around here?" Boyd asked.

"Si. I will go to the kitchen and find out what we can eat," Maldanado replied.

Then the other Rangers came around the corner of the mess hall. They were glad to see Sullivan and Boyd.

"Well, we wondered when you two would get back, and if you would," said Ben Warner.

"We made it," Sullivan answered.

"By the skin of our teeth," Boyd added.

"Did you get him?" asked Ben Long.

"I was close. Real close. Had my knife and pistol in his face, but then another pistol was pressing on the back of my neck. So, no I didn't get him. Me and Boyd just came over here to eat supper. I'm going back . . . ."

"And me too," Boyd interrupted.

". . . . and we'll get him this time."

"Don't y'all need some help?"

"No," Sullivan replied quickly. "It ain't legal. So just the two of us will go. I want you men to go on to Brownsville and wait there. Ya can't stay around here forever. Wait there a reasonable amount of time. If we don't get back, then you go on to Austin. Just tell'em, we, uh, ... died in the line of duty. In Texas. Not Mexico. Where's the food?"

Chapter 34

The next day, Sullivan, Boyd, and Maldanado rested, cleaned their weapon, ate as much food as they could, brushed down the borrowed Mexican horses, and gathered supplies of food, bullets, and extra canteens for the trip back to Mexico.

This time Sullivan was determined to get the General, Fernando De Vega, if it was the last thing he ever did. And it very well could be. He did not kid himself about that. He knew the danger of three men against who knew how many of De Vega's men.

They set out early the following day. The sun was coming up in the east, and it was good to make some miles before it got baking hot high.

They paused at the edge of the river for the usual and much needed drink for the horses.

"I want us to go back the way we came," Sullivan said, "right by that place where they killed our horses. I got to have my Sharps, and I want my own saddle if I can get it. I need that rifle bad. Besides I love it, whether I get to use it this time or not."

"Reckon how many men De Vega's got left?" asked Boyd. "We killed that eighteen and then some at the first fight we had with them, so we must have eliminated maybe thirty of 'em."

Turning to Maldanado, Sullivan asked, "What ya think?"

"I say he got maybe ten or twenty. I always thought he had about forty to fifty. Nothing we cannot handle."

"I like a positive attitude. Let's go."

They splashed their way across the river to the other side.

Close to noon they crossed the hills, and then made their way along the flat country. By three o'clock they came to the small hills with the large boulders where their horses lay. They dismounted and looked at them.

Sullivan pulled a small shovel out from under his pack behind his saddle.

"You gonna bury that horse?" Boyd asked, with a half laugh.

"I gonna dig up under him enough to get my rifle out. Then I'm gonna keep on digging until I can get my saddle off of'im. The cartridges for that Sharps are in those saddle bags, both sides, along with other stuff I just might need."

Sullivan walked over to the horse, and got down on his knees. He began pulling the dirt from under him, hoping to remove enough to get his rifle and the saddle.

The horses had been dead for a couple of days. They were getting pretty ripe. It was not a pleasant thing Sullivan was doing, but he had to do it, unpleasant or not.

An hour later, Sullivan was sitting on a boulder cleaning his Sharps rifle. It was good to have his old friend back. They had traveled many miles together and faced many enemies. When he was done, he leaned the rifle against the boulders and began cleaning his saddle.

Once he was through with that, he took the other saddle off his horse and replaced it with his own.

"Happy now?" asked Boyd.

"What do you think?"

"I'd say you're pretty happy for a man who just might be ridin' to his death."

"You're goin' with me whatever happens and wherever I go."

"Let's hope it's either Austin or Heaven and not Hell."

"I prefer the first two. Let's ride."

The three men mounted up and headed off toward General De Vega's hacienda. They knew they would not make it there that day.

Late in the afternoon, they came to a small river. It was a good place to camp for the night.

First, they let their horses drink. Then they tied them to small trees, took off the saddles, and place them near the water. They gathered enough fire wood to last the night. They built a fire between the three saddles, fried bacon, and heated a can of beans. They made coffee and drank all of it.

Just as it was getting dark, Sullivan said, "I'll take the first watch. Boyd, I'll wake you at midnight or thereabouts."

"Does thereabouts mean a little later maybe?"

"Yep. And it may mean a little earlier."

"All right."

Boyd and Maldanado settled down and pulled their blankets up over them. They were both asleep fairly quickly.

Sullivan watched the fire. As was so often the case, the little flames reminded him of how he set his farm house on fire when he left it back in Georgia. His wife and son were dead. He had come home from the war to nothing and no one. That had brought him to Texas, and he somehow fell into being a Texas Ranger. He wondered about the mystery of life, how one event leads to another and then another. One road you go down leads to another road even when a man had little interest in being on any road at all. Then he found Josephine Wells and married her. They had a wonderful life in Fort Worth – until she was murdered. In the midst of that part of his life, he discovered Constance had not died after all. Much to his surprise and shock, she and her husband bought the ranch Josephine had owned. He met Constance. Her husband was killed. Then she just disappeared, gone from his life again. If only he could find her. If. Life was full of ifs. If he had found her in Georgia, he would be a dirt farmer still, and a happy one at that.

He looked at the moon and counted the stars as the hours dragged by. Maybe he would wake up Boyd sooner than later. Boyd would not care.

Sullivan stood up and walked over to the horses to check on them. They had for a few minutes seemed nervous. He wanted to know what it was that disturbed them.

As he rubbed his horse, he suddenly heard a noise behind him!

Someone was running at him!

He turned around just as an arm with a knife came down at him!

He threw up his left arm to block the knife and took hold of his attacker's right arm with his right hand! He then reached over that right arm and grasped his left arm bending back the attacker's arm until he dropped the knife!

The man kicked up his left knee striking Sullivan!

They fell to the ground and rolled toward the river!

When they scrambled to their feet, they jumped at each other, taking hold, twisting, turning, and then falling in the water!

Sullivan still could not make out who it was. It was too dark and he was too busy to worry about his identity.

Sullivan was able to pulled his own knife out of his boot! He rammed into the gut of his assailant!

The man fell limp. Sullivan eased him down into the water.

"Boyd! Maldanado! Come here!"

Roused out of their sleep, the two men jumped up and ran to Sullivan.

"Hell's bells!" Boyd said. "What in the world?"

"I don't know," Sullivan replied. "You two take him to the fire. Let's see what we got. He wore me out quick."

They dragged the man over close to the fire so they could see him. Sullivan followed them, pushing his wet hair out of his face and back up on his head. They rolled him over, his face in the light.

"Apache," Maldanado said.

"What's he doin' here?" Boyd asked.

"He is here to steal horses. He is not alone. There are others. Get out of the light."

They hurried over away from the light, moving near the river.

"Two choices," Maldanado said. "We wait here for an attack by who knows how many of them, or we get out of here while we can without horses and our hair."

"Saddle up," Sullivan replied.

Chapter 35

They kicked out the fire, jumped on their horses, and bounded across the river, the water splashing up in all directions.

They rode hard and fast for a couple of miles. Then they stopped to listen.

"They are coming," Maldanado said.

"We'll run till the sun is up," Sullivan said. "Then we'll kill 'em."

They were off riding hard again, not knowing how many Indians were after them. They had no time to wonder or worry about that. It could wait until the right time. The object now was to stay alive until daylight.

As they rode through the darkness, Sullivan was thinking ahead. There was a big problem they were facing. They were beyond the hills now. There would be no good place for an ambush, nothing to hide behind, no way to protect themselves. He had to think of something.

After a couple of hours, they stopped to rest the horses.

"They are still back there," Maldanado said. "They will not stop."

"What do they want?" asked Boyd. "Our horses?"

"Si."

"Well, relax, Boys," Sullivan replied. "These ain't our horses. These horses belong to those Mexicans who ain't with us no more."

"I feel better already," Boyd quipped.

"You gonna feel dead if we don't get movin'. Let's get out of here."

On they raced through the darkness, hoping they were staying well ahead of the war party of Apache horse thieves.

They kept stopping at intervals to rest the horses; they were trusting they would not kill them by riding them to death.

Finally, the sky began to lighten up. It was almost dawn. If they were ever going to find a place for an ambush, it had to be soon.

Sullivan saw a gradual rise straight ahead. They stopped to look around.

"Look up there. I could be sittin' up there on that high place waitin' on them, daring them to come on."

"Are you all right, Sullivan?"

"Look off to each side approaching that place. The land slants down on both sides, maybe to little gulleys. One of ya get on one side, down low. The other on the other side over there. I'll be up there waiting on them. When they see me, they will most likely stop for a moment to look at what they're seeing. They won't believe it at first. But then will want to come get me. As soon as they begin to move toward me, I charge straight at them, shocking them again. When I start firing my Winchester at them, that's when y'all come up out of the lower sides there and charge into them from the left and the right. When I empty my Winchester, I'll drop it and pull out my pistol as I move right in amongst'em. We don't know how many there are, but there couldn't be a large body of 'em. How does that sound?"

"It sounds like suicide," Boyd answered.

"Got a better idea?"

"None."

"You?" Sullivan said to Maldanado.

"No idea."

"Let's do it. Take ya places, and we'll wait on 'em. Shouldn't be too terribly long. Good luck."

"Thanks," Boyd replied unenthusiastically.

As Boyd and Maldanado split off to the right and left, Sullivan rode on toward the rise out in front of him. Once there, he jumped down off his horse to let him rest and nibble on the few grass sprouts there were along the top of the rise.

He stretched his legs and began walking around in little circles. He had been on that horse all night and needed to get his blood flowing again. There had not been many times when he had ridden that long and that far without a good long break.

Looking back behind where they had come from, he wondered how many Indians there really were. He was hoping he was right in thinking it would not be that many.

The sun was coming on up. The day was brightening now so that he could see very well back across the long flat plain they had come over. The Indians would be coming that way soon. They would be riding hard and fast.

Sullivan took his binoculars out of his saddle bag. He scanned the horizon. Nothing yet. But it can't be long, he was thinking.

He put the strap of his binoculars over the horn of his saddle as he removed a canteen. He drank a few sips of water.

He pulled out his pistol, making sure it was fully loaded. Then he checked his Winchester to make sure it was as well.

He was thinking about charging the Apaches and emptying the rifle on them. He hoped when he dropped it to the ground, he did not break the stock. Maybe he could let it drop flat and not hit on the stock or barrel. It would all be happening too quickly to be sure about that. He knew it.

He was beginning to have that funny feeling in his stomach the way any sane man would feel. He had to take a deep breath and relax.

Sullivan walked back to his horse to get the binoculars again. He held them up and looked through them. He had put the canteen back across the saddle horn.

There it was far out in the distance – that little cloud of dust growing a little bigger with every second that passed.

The Apaches were coming as sure as the day is long. They would be real close real soon.

Boyd stood by his horse unable to see anything down in the low place where he was waiting. He wondered how long it would be. More importantly, he wondered if Sullivan's plan would work. A thing like that could get a man killed. And that right quick.

On the other side, Maldanado waited also. He knew the Apaches better than Sullivan and Boyd. He knew things about them they did not know. The Comanches were the finest horse soldiers anywhere. They always attacked on horseback. Not so with the Apaches. They did not attack on horseback. They always dismounted and took cover, ran for cover, and then they would attack on foot, running, weaving, dodging, shooting. He forgot to mention that to Sullivan, but he should have done it. Maybe he better go tell him before it was too late.

Maldanado tied his horse to a scrub. He slowly and careful made his way back up the little rise before him. When he reached the top, he peeped up over the edge without exposing himself. He could see Sullivan on the rise looking at something. He turned and looked back where Sullivan was looking. Too late! They were coming fast!

He ran back down and got on his horse.

Sullivan put his binoculars back in his saddle bag, pulled out his Winchester, mounted his horse, and waited.

Chapter 36

It won't be long now, Sullivan was thinking. They'll see me coming at them and the fight will be on. Here they come.

"All right, Mexican horse. We gonna see what you're made of."

He kicked the horse in his ribs on both sides and charged down the rise.

The Apaches saw him. They stopped where they were, a hundred yards or so out in front of him.

Sullivan knew they knew he was not alone. They knew there were three of them.

They split into two groups, maybe six, seven in each group, he could not tell.

They hurried off to the right and the left, heading down into the low places where Boyd and Maldanado were hiding.

What now? What to do?

Sullivan halted his horse and threw up his Winchester to his shoulder!

He started firing at them!

Bang!

Bang!

He hit none!

But he wanted Boyd and Maldanado to come up out of the low areas for they were about to be overrun!

They both came riding fast to where he was!

They saw no Apaches!

"What!" Boyd exclaimed.

"They're heading to where y'all were!"

"They are on foot now!" Maldanado yelled. "A detail I forgot to tell about Apaches!"

"Up the rise!" Sullivan shouted, as he whirled his horse around!

They rode fast up the rise. Wh

en they reached the top, they quickly dismounted, and Boyd took their horses down the other side and tied them to scrub. Then he came up to where Sullivan and Maldanado were waiting.

"What now?" Boyd asked.

They both looked at Maldanado.

"They will be creeping crawling up along both sides."

"Do we go meet'em or wait?" Boyd asked.

"I never like waiting," Sullivan responded. "Let's go introduce ourselves."

Then he turned and said, as he started off toward the right side, "Let's stay together. A better chance that way. We'll take this side first. The others will then come running, I guess. We'll be ready."

They hurried down the right side of the rise and then went down into the lower area.

As soon as they got there, they saw the Apaches coming around a bend.

Sullivan dropped to his knees and began firing his Winchester!

Bang!

Bang!

Two Indians hit the ground!

Boyd and Maldanado, standing behind him and a little to his right, started firing!

Bang!

Bang!

Bang!

Bang!

Two more fell to the ground!

Here came five more running fast and firing their rifles!

Bang!

Bang!

Bang!

Bang!

They were on Sullivan, Boyd, and Maldanado before they could shoot them!

Sullivan fired at point blank range!

Bang!

No good!

He took his rifle by the barrel and swung it at the Apache, striking him across his face!

He fell to the ground.

Sullivan shot him!

Bang!

Another jumped on him, knocking him to the ground!

They rolled in the dirt as Sullivan pulled out his knife and stabbed him in his abdomen!

Boyd and Maldanado were in similar fights!

Boyd pulled out his pistol and started shooting wildly!

Pow!

Pow!

Pow!

Pow!

He killed the others, one of them falling across Maldanado as they were rolling on the ground!

Sullivan raced up the slope to the level ground!

"They're comin'!"

He began firing his Winchester at them!

Bang!

Bang!

Bang!

Bang!

Boyd and Maldanado quickly joined him!

Bang!

Bang!

Bang!

Bang!

Then there was silence. Six dead Apaches lay on the ground.

"Let's get out of here," Sullivan said.

They walked up the rise slowly, neither of them saying anything. They knew they were lucky to get through that fight and still have their hair.

They got on their horses and rode away, still saying nothing at all.

Chapter 37

The day was now overcast and not as hot as it had been. This was good for the men and the horses. They could make better time without worrying about hurting the animals.

There was no need to be in a hurry except that Sullivan was wanting to get on with it and get the job done. He was worn down from being in Mexico, and there was no place like Texas for him. Boyd felt the same way, though neither of them said it for fear of offending Maldanado and his family. They would just keep it to themselves. Complaining would do no good anyway.

On they rode, mile after dusty mile, hoping the light clouds would produce a little rain, even a little shower. But they were not that kind of clouds.

The battle with the Apaches had been another close call. There had been too many of those. How many more could they face without their luck running out, Sullivan wondered. But as he thought about it, he knew his life had been a series of close calls dating back to his time in the war and his first days in Texas.

Finally, they were able to look ahead and see the village where Maldanado's family lived.

"Will not be long now!" Maldanado shouted.

Soon they stopped in front of the home of Maldanado's brother.

Hearing the horses, Fernando came out to greet them. He was followed closely by Maria.

"Ah, I see you returned. I wondered what had happened to you."

"I will tell you the complete story after we wash up," Anton Maldanado replied.

"You remember Mister Sullivan, and this is his friend and now my friend, William Boyd."

"We are pleased to meet you, Mister Boyd and glad to see you Mister Sullivan. We are

pleased to have you both in our home."

Boyd smiled and nodded his head and looked at Sullivan.

"We thank ya for yore hospitality," Sullivan responded.

"I will prepare food for you," Maria said, as she went back inside.

Having washed their hands and faces, the two brothers talked while Sullivan and Boyd sat out back at the table.

"What ya think our chances will be?" Boyd asked.

Sullivan smiled and almost laughed, as he said, "We won't know till we get there. But I will say this, we have greatly reduced the size of his so-called cattle thievin' army."

"That we have. We really have done that."

"No idea, of course, how many men he's got left."

"We'll have to reduce'em some more," Boyd replied.

Soon Maria brought out the food. Sullivan and Boyd were joined at the table by the brothers.

Fernando poured wine into four cups as the other three began eating. They did not know how hungry they were until they saw the food. The meal was roasted chicken, beans, peppers, tomatoes, onions, and tortillas.

Maria came back out to check on them.

"This is really good," Boyd said to her. "Appreciate it."

"Me too," Sullivan added.

"Si. Me as well," Anton responded, with a big smile.

"Glad you like. There is more. Just let me know," she replied.

"Si. We will, we will," Anton said.

After the meal, Sullivan and Boyd walked out front and down the little street while the three family members visited with each other.

"Boyd, I been thinkin'."

"Yeah?"

"What about we hit'em at dawn with the sun to our backs? Me sneakin' in after mid-night didn't work out all that well. Wasn't a bad plan, but I just got caught. I don't know if he'll be expectin' us to return or not. He knows why we're here, to get him. I expect he might have a heavy guard at night, more than last time. With the sun comin' up, they just might relax some, and maybe others won't be stirrin' around much yet."

"That sounds good to me. Whatever you think."

"I want us to go over in the mornin' and have a look. I'd like to know how things are before we go chargin' in there."

"Good idea."

After his usual restless night, Sullivan was up early. His stirring around woke up Boyd.

"You must be anxious to get on with it," Boyd said, as he yawned.

"I guess so. Couldn't sleep for thinking about it."

"I smell coffee."

"Yeah," Sullivan replied. "Maria's up. She'll have something we can eat."

The two Rangers put on their boots and shirts and went into the kitchen of the little house.

"Good morning," Maria said. "I have coffee. And I am cooking some eggs for you. We have chickens. Lay good eggs. And I fix tortillas for you and beans and tomatoes. That good?"

"That sounds wonderful," Sullivan answered.

"Did you sleep well?"

"Yes. Very well."

"And you Mister Boyd?"

"Oh, yes. Very good."

They stepped outside and sat down at the table. A faint light was just appearing in the eastern sky.

Maria brought out two cups of coffee.

"There," she said, as she placed them on the table before the two men. They thanked her.

Both men picked up the cups and blew into them, hoping to cool down the boiling coffee a little.

Soon Maria came back with two plates containing the food. They ate quickly.

When they were finished, they took the plates and cups back inside and gave them to Maria.

"Tell Anton and Fernando me and Boyd are going for a little ride to take a look at that hacienda. We'll be back later in the day."

"Si. Be very careful," she said.

They both nodded their heads.

Soon they were on their way west. They rode hard and fast.

They stopped when they got close enough to see the wall and the village.

"See that little hill off to the right there?" Sullivan asked.

"Yeah."

"We'll go up there where we can get a good look at what's happenin'. Maybe."

"All right."

When they came to the hill, they stopped and dismounted. Sullivan took his binoculars from his saddle bags. They climbed up the hill, and when they reached the top, they bent down low.

Sullivan put the binoculars up to his eyes and scanned the entire area before them. Then he handed them to Boyd.

"Here. Take a look."

Boy looked all around for a few moments.

"What was I lookin' for?"

"See anything out of the ordinary?"

"I don't guess so, but then I don't know what ordinary is around here and especially there."

"I don't either," Sullivan said, with a smile. "But I see that big house is still there. I tried to burn it down. But I don't reckon I did."

"Reckon not. It's there."

"That's really all I wanted to know."

"Now you know," Boyd said.

"Yep."

"Well then, let's get out of here."

They hurried back down the hill to the horses.

When they reached the Maldanado's home, later in the morning, they shared with Anton what they had seen and what the plan would be.

Chapter 38

Long before sunup, the three men left on their journey to the village where De Vega lived in his large hacienda. This time they would kill him. Sullivan was determined they would be successful or die trying.

When they reached the outskirts of the village, they paused for a moment.

In a low voice, Sullivan spoke to Boyd and Maldanado.

"Look, I think the best way in is still over that back wall. Maldanado, you stay out with the horses. Boyd, you come with me, and you make sure we have a way to get back over that wall. I'll run and make sure that back door is so we can get in it. When we get inside, shoot anything and anybody that moves, but no women and children. Questions?"

Both men shook their heads.

"All right, let's ease on up and around to the back."

They were still under the cover of darkness, though the sky was beginning to lighten up as the sun slowly made its way toward the horizon back behind them. By the time they were in position, they would be able to see clearly.

They quietly went around the corner of the wall and stopped when they reached the back of it.

Maldanado held the three horses as Sullivan and Boyd stood up on theirs and pulled themselves up to the top of the wall. Then as they sat there, they turned so they could ease themselves down to the ground on the other side.

They crouched down for a few moments, waiting to see if there was anyone outside or near the back door. They saw no one and heard nothing.

Sullivan raced to the back door, as Boyd got a ladder in place for their return over the wall.

The door was unlocked as before. He slowly pulled it open and waited for Boyd. When Boyd joined him, they stepped inside. They smelled the odor from the fires, but they had been quickly put out and there was very little real damage they could tell.

As they slipped down the hall toward the stairs that led up the second floor, a man in the front of the house opened fire at them!

Pow!

Pow!

They ducked down and returned fire, killing him!

Pow!

Pow!

Pow!

"Up the stairs quick!" Sullivan said, as he led the way.

When they reached the top floor, they were met with more gunfire!

Pow!

Pow!

Pow!

And someone fired a shotgun at them tearing away a hunk of the corner of the wall they were looking around!

Boom!

There at the top of the stairs, Sullivan laid down and lunged out onto the floor of the hall firing rapidly!

Pow!

Pow!

Two men fell to the floor in front of him twenty feet away!

He jumped to his feet and motioned for Boyd to follow him up the hall toward the front of the house. That is where De Vega's bedroom was located.

They heard someone running up the stairs behind them! They ducked down close to the floor!

A man jumped out in the hall, not seeing them at first!

They dropped him!

Pow!

Pow!

There was more commotion downstairs! Men were rushing into the house and coming toward the stairs! They would soon be coming up them! They could not tell how many there were, but it was more than two or three!

While Boyd quickly reloaded his pistol, Sullivan stuffed his under his belt. He picked up the double-barreled shotgun and opened the breach, dropping the empty shells to the floor. He reached into the pockets of one of the dead men, searching for shells. Then he saw the man was wearing a shell belt around his neck and under one arm. He pulled out two shells, placed them in the shotgun, and cocked back both hammers. He held the shotgun in his left hand and with his right he unbuckled the belt and pulled it off the man. He slung it over his left shoulder.

Men were coming up the stairs!

"Watch that door!" he said to Boyd, as he quickly pointed his thumb back over his shoulder toward the bedroom.

Then Sullivan jumped up and ran to the top of the stairs!

The men in front were two-thirds of the way up them!

Boom!

Boom!

Two men were blown almost apart as they fell backward causing the others to stumble back down the stairs.

Sullivan reloaded quickly.

Boom!

Boom!

Two more men fell dead!

One man crawled out from under dead bodies and slid back up the hall toward the front door.

Sullivan raced down the stairs, reloading the shotgun as he did!

He turned the corner and saw the man almost reaching the front door!

Boom!

Boom!

The man fell against the door!

Reloading again, Sullivan whirled around making sure there was no one coming in the back door behind him. He did not see anyone.

He stepped over the pile of dead men and went back upstairs. He did not see Boyd in the hall, but a lamp had been lit in De Vega's bedroom. When he got to the room, he looked in the door.

Boyd was standing by the bed. The same naked young woman was on the bed, sitting up on her knees. She held a sheet up in front of herself.

"Where is he? De Vega! Where?"

She did not seem to understand what Sullivan was asking her.

"She don't speak English," Boyd said.

"She knows what I'm askin'. Where?" he yelled, as he pointed to where De Vega had been in the bed.

She pointed out the door and waved her arm toward the front of the house.

Sullivan walked out in the hall to the front where there was a large window. It was open. He returned to the bedroom.

"He's gone."

"She can't tell us where," Boyd said.

"I bet there's someone here in this village who can tell us."

"Who?" Boyd asked.

"Let's go to church."

Chapter 39

"I'm goin' out the front door," Sullivan said, as he and Boyd got to the bottom of the stairs. "You go get Maldanado and the horses and meet me out front, but y'all keep yore eyes peeled real good. May be some of his men still around."

Sullivan walked to the front door. Before going outside, he looked out in all directions. He saw no one anywhere. Then he ran to the front gate. Obviously, the people of the village had heard all the shooting for there was no one in the streets, no old men, no women, no children, and no dogs. Even the dogs ran. Then he walked on through the gate. He looked up and down the street again. Still no one.

Boyd and Maldanado came around the corner of the wall. When they stopped, Sullivan got on his horse. He pointed to the church at the end of the street.

They slowly rode down the street toward the church, still being cautious, making sure there was no one on a roof or behind a wagon or standing in a door waiting to kill them.

When they got to the church, they dismounted. Sullivan and Boyd walked to the front door and Maldanado held the horses.

They looked inside and saw the priest wiping dust off the altar rail. They walked inside toward him. He looked up and saw them.

The priest was tall and thin. He appeared to be an older man, maybe the same age as De Vega. He was not wearing the usual brown robe, but was dressed in black pants and a white shirt. He was not Mexican either. It was not easy to tell what he was and if he was really the priest. Sullivan decided to ask if he was the priest just to make sure.

"You the Padre?"

"I am."

"Padre, we need to talk to you," Sullivan said, when they got closer to him.

"It's you."

"Yeah. It's us. I see you speak English."

"Yes, and Spanish, French, and Latin. I did my schooling in Rome."

"Well, good."

"You are the men doing all the shooting?"

"Yes, we are."

"Did you leave anyone in the village alive?"

"We only shot the men who were shootin' at us. Everybody else is fine."

"Did you kill the General?"

"No. That's why we're here."

"He is not here."

"I know that. We wanna know where he went."

"I will tell you what I think. I came here as a young man. The General and his brother were about my age. We became friends quickly. They both grew up here of course. I buried their parents. The General went off to the army. His brother became a rancher south of here. He has a very big ranch. Antonio and his brother Carlos were good boys and fine young men. But time and the world both work on people, don't they? The army made Antonio hungry for power and wealth, and then Carlos wanted wealth also. They wanted to escape the poor conditions of this village. They did. Carlos is a very rich man. Antonio as well. When Antonio came back here, after leaving the army, he did so much for the people here. He has fed and clothed them and their children. But both of them have been corrupted by wealth and the gaining of it. The problem is they never have enough. There is never enough. When they get more, they want more. I have talked with them many times, trying to tell them there can be no good outcome for them. But they would not listen to me. Now I am afraid that day has come for them. Antonio is with Carlos now, I am sure. His ranch is straight south, about ten miles. Just who are you anyway?"

"We're Texas Rangers," Sullivan said. "We've come to stop what De Vega has been doin' in Texas."

"Are you going to kill them?"

"We intend to, if they don't kill us."

"Why must it be this way?"

"There is no other way."

"There must be."

"Not with men like that."

"You could take him to Texas to stand trial?"

"I got no witness, no evidence, nothin'."

"I hate to see my brothers die this way."

"Don't look, Padre. You won't be there no how. Just come bury them tomorrow. Or us."

"I will do just that. Blessings on you both and on them as well. Peace be with you," the priest said, as he made the sign of the cross in front of them.

"Thanks, Padre."

When they got back outside to the horses, Sullivan looked back down the street.

"Let's go back to that house and get some of their weapons. We just might need'em. We'll get a few pistols and another rifle each and their ammo. Maldanado, you get that shotgun and the belt with the shells. We might need it. You use it. Say, you know where that place is, the ranch?"

"I do know. We find it no trouble."

"How many men they gonna have there?"

"Carlos has a good many vaqueros. But most will be out with the herds. But he will have some there for protection, I am sure."

"Let's go," Sullivan said.

When they got to the hacienda, they tied their horses outside and then walked through the gate to the house. They went inside and started collecting some of the guns.

Sullivan heard one of the men at the foot of the stairs groan. He took the man's pistol from him and shot him in the head. Then he dropped the pistol on him.

"Here, you keep this one," Sullivan said, as he pointed to another on the floor.

He picked up two more pistols, stuffed one of them under his belt, opposite his own, and then pushed the other down in his right boot on the outside. Then he picked up a Winchester, much like his own.

"You Boys ready?" he asked.

Boyd said, "Yes," as he gathered three pistols and one rifle.

"Si," Maldanado replied, as he put the belt with shotgun shells over his head and one shoulder while holding the shotgun in his hand. He also had found an extra pistol.

"I think we're well armed," Sullivan said, as he walked toward the front door, the others behind him.

Outside they got on their horses and headed south out of the village.

"Take us there," Sullivan said to Maldanado.

Chapter 40

Maldanado came riding hard and fast back to Sullivan and Boyd.

"I found the hacienda. It about two mile ahead. It is large and brick, but no wall around it. There are two large barns about fifty yards out front and down to the right of it with two large corrals and all connected to each other. Not see many men."

Sullivan looked at Boyd and back at Maldanado. He thought a moment and then spoke.

"You know they know we're comin'. I'm guessing there are some in both barns, and maybe hiding on top of that house. What ya think?"

Boyd spit on the ground.

"I think you're right about that. So what do we do?"

"I say we circle around to the back of the house and go chargin' in as fast as we can.

They'll be lookin' out this way, expectn' us, but we'll come up on their blind side so fast they won't have time to spot us and get off a shot. We'll go straight for the back door. They got a back door?"

"Si. They have back door."

"We'll just ride right into the house. That back door gonna be open or closed?"

"It is open now. Big. Room for horses to go in."

"If it ain't open, then Maldanado, you go to it first and open it. We'll go by you right on in. Shoot everythin' that moves, but no women and children."

"When the shootin' starts, we'll have trouble," Boyd said. "Everybody in those barns and on the house will come runnin' at us."

"I'm countin' on it. We'll shoot'em one at a time. We got plenty of guns and plenty of ammo. Ready?"

"I'm ready."

"Si."

Maldanado led them around to the west. They went along the edge of trees for more than a mile. They cut across pasture land, stayed in low places, and tried to not create any silhouettes against the shy. They rode by small herds of cattle, all unattended.

Soon they were behind the large house. It was three hundred yards away. They paused for a moment. They could not see anyone looking their way.

"Well, this is it. Good luck, Boys," Sullivan said. "Hope to see ya on the other side."

Sullivan held a Winchester in his left hand, as did Boyd. Maldanado had the shotgun in his right hand.

"Let's go!"

They kicked their horses in their sides and off they rode toward the house. They could see there was no one at the back door for some strange reason. And that door was wide open.

In a few brief minutes, they were at the house! Sullivan's horse jumped up on the short porch and bounded through the door! Boyd and Maldanado were right behind him!

A man sitting by the door just inside was startled awake!

Bang!

Up the long wide hall they rode!

Two men were standing at the staircase! They quickly held up their rifles!

Bang!

Bang!

Their rifles hit the floor just before they did!

Sullivan and Boyd charged to the front of the house!

Maldanado saw two men rushing down the stairs!

Boom!

Boom!

They rolled to the bottom of the stairs!

Maldanado jumped down off of his horse and stood at the bottom of the stairs expecting other men to come down them. He quickly reloaded the shotgun.

There were five shocked men standing at the front door!

They turned around and looked back down the hall!

Bang!

Bang!

Bang!

Bang!

Bang!

Sullivan and Boyd jumped off their horses!

The dead men were piled all over each other!

"You stay here and guard this door," Sullivan said. "I'm goin' upstairs and find'em."

He put his Winchester back in the saddle scabbard. He pulled two pistols from under his belt.

"Here they come!" Boyd shouted.

"How many?"

"Seven or eight!"

"You handle them!"

"Sure," Boyd muttered sarcastically.

"Keep an eye out. There'll be more."

"Wonderful."

Boyd knocked the glass out of the front door!

He started firing his Winchester!

Bang!

Bang!

Bang!

Bang!

Bang!

Bang!

Bang!

Seven dead men lay at the beginning of the flagstone walkway that led to the steps of the front porch. Only one of them had managed to fire a shot.

Boyd reloaded his Winchester.

Sullivan stood at the foot of the stairs. He looked at the dead men there, and then looked at Maldanado.

"Keep an eye on that back door. They'll be comin' in there."

"Si."

Sullivan slowly crept up the stairs. When he reached the top, he stopped to listen. He heard nothing. He looked around the corner. There was no one there.

A man jumped out of a room on his left twenty feet away!

Pow!

Sullivan dropped him in the doorway. It was not De Vega. But he did not look like a hired man. He was dressed too well. A finely trimmed mustache was across his upper lip. No other facial hair. It must be the brother, Sullivan thought.

Sullivan turned around to be sure there was no one behind him. The hall was empty.

Bang!

Bang!

Bang!

Boom!

Boom!

The shots came from the first floor. The boys were busy down there.

Sullivan slipped along the wall to his left. De Vega had to be there somewhere.

There was a door on the right, twelve or thirteen feet away. He must be in there. Is he going to jump out of it firing away? Only one way to find out. He walked to the slightly open door and pushed it open.

Then he ducked!

Pow!

A bullet whizzed over his head!

Pow!

Pow!

Sullivan's two bullets hit De Vega in the chest!

He fell across the bed.

Boom!

One last dead man who tried to come in the backdoor.

A silence fell over the house. It was over. Sullivan left the room and went back to the first floor.

Chapter 41

They led their horses out the front door and down the steps off the porch.

"Well, that's it, Boys," Sullivan said.

"What about all these dead men lying around inside and out here?" Boyd asked.

"We gonna bury them or what?"

"There's women and old men around here. They'll take care of it. Just leave'em lay."

They mounted up and headed back toward Maldanado's home in the little village. As they left, they rode slowly. There was no hurry now, no reason to rush, no reason to be careful. Their work was done.

Sullivan had finished the job, had completed what he came to do. But there was no feeling of accomplishment, no satisfaction with a job well done. He was glad it was over, but he was not happy. It was just more killing. He had done a lot of killing. It was never anything to be proud of, no matter who it was, whether it was Comanches, Apaches, Comancheros, bank robbers, or wild killers. It was all the same. It always left a deep empty feeling, a sense of dread, a strange kind of guilt about keeping himself alive by ending the lives of other human beings. But that was the job, always the same, the same job. Just kill them with the perfect hatred he had learned to feel and act on. Period.

The three men rode for miles without saying a word. Finally, Boyd could stand it no longer.

"Hey, Sullivan. Ya think ya might look up that Augusta Browning we left back in Corpus Christie? She was good lookin', and she seemed to have an eye on you maybe when we left there."

"Nope. But the men are waitin' on us in Brownsville. Let's go to south Texas, Boys."

Sullivan spurred his horse and moved out ahead.

But he did have one woman on his mind. Constance was out there somewhere in Texas. Maybe he could find her. He knew you never stop loving someone the way he loved her.

The End